First published by Joe Boyle, 2022.

Paperback ISBN-13: 979-8-75-889962-5

Edited and typeset by MJV Literary Author Services.
Published in the United Kingdom.

RIPLEY!

The Aromatic Adventures of the World's Smelliest Dog

Joe Boyle

Dedication

For three brave people, Milly, Erin and Jacob, with all my love.

ONE

Himself

THE FAMILY HAD no idea what they were *really* getting when they picked up the cute pup from the Animal Rescue people.

They named him Ripley, and he was everything they'd ever dreamed of in a dog: curly, lively, bright eyes, a waggy tail and (in Dad-speak) "a leg at each corner".

Twelve-year-old twins Jacob and Erin, and big sister Milly, fell for him straight away, especially Jacob, who was a nutter for animals and often said that he wished he had been born one. Erin told him that he *had* been, but he just didn't realize it!

Ripley quickly became a full family member, and so his full name became Ripley Wigglesworth-Winterbottom, which is a mouthful for *anyone* to say, but since he would never be called upon to *say* it (most dogs don't), that was okay.

But right now he was the reason that they, the family, were standing in the front garden, in the withering rain, noses held and sucking in air like divers rescued from the deep. While he, Ripley, watched them through the window, his head at a puzzled angle, from the back of the sofa in the living room.

It had all begun so well. Jacob had lost no time in teaching him all the new-puppy tricks:

* sit…

* lie down…

* paw…

* make a cup of tea (just kidding there)…

* spin…

* bark in Russian (what?)…

*fetch…

He liked "fetch" so much that he'd fetch things he hadn't been asked to fetch, just so that you could ask him to fetch them again.

Right then, at the start, they were a happy little family, with everyday happy-little-family problems, for which there was always a solution. But all that was set to change...

Mum was a dinner lady at Jacob and Erin's school, and Dad had an office job, which he hated so much that he almost hated *hating* it. To take his mind off his horrible job, Dad had a hobby which involved all things strange, weird, mysterious and unexplained:

* flying saucers…

* mysterious happenings…

* ghostly sightings…

* line dancing…

and:

*strange coincidences…

In fact, he was so anxious for strange coincidences to happen that he'd find something "strange" in any ordinary coincidence, even if there wasn't anything remotely strange about it, like the day that the postman and the milkman arrived at the door at the same time. "How often do you suppose *that* would happen?" he kept saying through his toast and marmalade, as though the postman and the milkman were planning a joint milk-and-paper attack any day now.

Ripley loved everybody and everybody loved him, and

what happened next really, *really* wasn't his fault.

He had an appetite like an elephant! No, I don't mean he actually stripped leaves off of trees and stuffed them in his mouth. No, he just ate and ate and ate *soooo* much. And not just food! All pups chew things, like slippers and newspapers, but in Ripley's case he actually *ate* them, then looked around for more. Slippers in particular – any size, any colour (though red was his fave); hide them and he'd find them and eat them (except for the sole). He'd even been known to whip them off of people's feet while they were snoozing. Dad lost count of the times he woke up to find his slippers in pieces and Ripley burping.

He liked real food too, of course, and there was more than one day when a bacon tart or a string of sausages went mysteriously missing from the fridge. Dad staked out the fridge one night, hoping to see a spook that lived on bacon tarts, but instead he saw Ripley nosing open the fridge door. So, he put a lock on it (the fridge door, not Ripley's nose!). No more fridge food for him. BUT ends of rugs, T.V. remotes, books and money… if it was there and he came across it, he ate it.

For example, Dad had a hearing problem, so he had bought a very expensive pair of hearing aids – the sort you just slip into your ear and they were meant to be invisible. But not to Ripley they weren't. Okay, Dad should have known better than to put them aside on the toilet seat while he shaved, but this was before anybody knew what Ripley was really capable of; all Dad saw was Ripley's tail disappearing down the corridor from the bathroom, and an empty space where his hearing aids had been.

Milly tried to make a joke of it. "From now on," she said, "all we need to do is *whisper* Ripley's name, and if he's within twenty miles he'll be here like a shot, *ha ha ha*!"

But Dad didn't see the funny side of it, and he had a face like a wet week all that day, and the day after.

Still, naughty though he was, Ripley had their hearts, so they forgave him.

But, as they say, "watch this space"...

TWO

Poo

RIPLEY'S BREED WAS a mixture of Cocker Spaniel and Poodle. He was, in fact, a "Cockerpoo".

And that *could* have been a clue to what was about to happen, because it soon became as obvious as anything that the "cocker" wasn't half as prominent as the "poo"!

On a short walk, he could easily do anything up to five poos, and though the children were very good at cleaning the mess, funnily enough, it never became something that they actually looked forward to.

When Ripley was about six months old, on a cold Friday evening in December, the family were sitting around the television enjoying an episode of *I'm An Idiot, Please Lock Me Up*. They were watching a little-known celebrity D.J. called Billy Dripp trying to swallow a cupful of wriggly maggots, when the picture on the telly began to flicker. At the same time there came a smell.

Dad, with his suspicious face on, went to check the socket in the wall where the telly was plugged in. Maybe, he thought, the smell was the wires beginning to burn. But he never got that far! The smell, which had now grown to a full-blown pong, hit him like a brick in the face, and he reeled back with a look of horror.

Alarm spread as the others saw Dad, frozen in motion, mouth open and watery eyes staring into nothing. Then the pong hit *them* and they gasped, shrieked and fled the room fast, beaten to the door by Dad himself, leaving Ripley bewildered and alone.

"Shut the door!" shouted Mum, as they emptied into the hall.

"Shut it yourself!" shouted back Milly, as she bolted for the front garden.

It was Jacob who pulled his t-shirt up over his nose and slammed the lounge door, before streaking outside to the others grouped on the front lawn.

"What was that?!" gasped Milly, her eyes stinging.

Blank, bewildered looks went all around, from rain-streaked faces.

Then, from the other side of the window, Ripley gave a bark, his tongue hanging strap-like from an undeniable grin. Mum went pale, gasped and put a hand to her mouth. The others noticed.

"What??"

She gulped and pointed. "It was him!" she cried. "Ripley! It was him!"

They shared a look.

"Not possible!" said Milly, in disbelief. "No dog could make a stink like that!"

Everybody searched everybody else's wet, unbelieving face...

"Could it?"

She was right. No *ordinary* dog could have. But then, Ripley was fast showing that he was no ordinary dog.

THREE

Nightmare

THE NEXT FEW weeks were spent trying to cope with Ripley's gastric maladjustment – that means an adjustment which is "mal", which is Spanish for "bad". And as for "gastric" – well, look it up in the dictionary (*but, take it from me, "gastric" does **not** mean a trick with gas!*).

First call was to the vet, who wasn't much help. He was quick to tell them that he'd never come across a case like this before, and hoped that he never would again. In three separate visits he prescribed three separate (and dead expensive) "remedies":

*"Pong-Go", at £350 a bottle!

Then:

*"Waftaway", costing £500 an ounce!

And after that:

*"Niff-Less", at £1000 a spoonful (a *teaspoon*, that is)!

None of them made any difference at all – except to the

family's bank balance.

Eventually, the vet had to ban Ripley from his surgery, because he had used up all the super-duper strength surgical masks that he, his staff, waiting clients and the gardener outside were forced to wear every time Ripley was brought in. He did, though, very kindly give one to each of the family and, with a look of pity, wished them good luck. The masks didn't completely block out the smell, but they gave everyone enough time to get somewhere else quick. It was up to the family now, to deal with the problem as best they could.

Mum tried Ripley on different foods, some very exotic, which had to be sent away for.

From Australia, she was able to get:

*"Chunky Ostrich Bites", which he liked but which didn't work (and Erin said they were making his neck longer)...

so, they tried:

*"Scrambled Gopher Ears", from somewhere that had too many gophers...

then, something called:

*"Liver and Marmalade Toasties". Yes, you read that correctly! From that, they learned that toasties with liver and marmalade should *never* be given to *any* living, breathing animal *or* human being, *even* your least-fave teacher or your worst enemy, *ever,* anywhere in the world or universe. Neither did they do anything for Ripley's problem…

Mum even tried bringing leftovers from the school dining hall:

*toad-in-the-hole…

*toad-out-of-the-hole…

*turkey twizzlers…

*soggy sago pudding (lots of this, as very few kids liked it)…

and:

*salad ('cos *no* kids liked it)…

Strangely enough, Ripley liked the salad, yet most dogs don't. He liked it so much that shortly after he tried to eat a green paper napkin, thinking it was a piece of lettuce, followed by Erin's red nose, left over from Red Nose Day, thinking it was a tomato.

She even gave him alphabetti spaghetti, with all the letters taken out which spelt pongy words like "poop", "bottom-burp", "niff" and "pong".

But nothing made the slightest difference.

She gave up when Milly asked her how she supposed school dinners – which weren't even fit for human consumption (in her opinion) – were going to cure a smelly dog.

Life was fast becoming a nightmare!

Walking him could be embarrassing, but if he happened to "do one" outside, they found that the pong could be blamed on the fumes of some passing car. They'd be talking to someone and it'd be like:

"Phew! Some of these exhausts don't half smell, don't they?"

And then, quickly:

"Well, it was nice talking to you. 'Bye."

Then smartly off, leaving whoever they had been talking to wondering if they needed a change of deodorant.

They began to realize just how bad it was getting when the postman began standing at the gate and throwing the letters, Frisbee-style, at the letterbox.

After six months of all this, the strain on the family was beginning to show...

FOUR

Shops

IT HAPPENED ON a Tuesday, on a fine, spring-blessed day...

Erin had brought the milk in off the doorstep and, having her hands full, had kicked the door closed behind her – or, at least she *thought* she had. She heard the click but the catch hadn't caught, and a breeze blew the door ajar as she walked away. Enter Ripley from the front lounge...

He'd only had one sock and a chew on an old slipper since he woken up, and he was looking forward to getting his teeth into his breakfast. He felt the breeze, looked and saw the door ajar. Unlike fridge doors, doors ajar were no problem to him, 'cos he knew they could be pawed open. In less than a second he was out and, for the first time ever, on the loose!

On leaving the gate he turned right instead of left. He knew that left led to the common, but right? *Who knows?*

Let's find out! With no lead to keep him in check, he found he could run when he felt like it, wander and jump, turn, or stop for as long as he wanted when he saw something interesting.

And right now, he was staring at something pretty interesting… But the cat had seen him first and was now sitting out of reach, on top of a gatepost. All he could do was throw a grump-growl, which ended in a "Yap!" as he went past.

His curiosity was up, and he knew that as long as he kept clear of those big, noisy things on wheels which went *"Beep-beep!"* he could go where no dog had gone before.

Little did he know that he was heading in the direction of town, and before long he hit the shops. He didn't know that they were shops; they were just buildings that people were going in and out of. But he gave each one a foody-sniff test, because he was hungry by now. One shop smelled like a garden and had flowers outside of it, so he did what he was used to doing in his own garden and peed on them. A very shouty, wavy-armed woman ran out of the shop and shooed him away, for no reason that *he* could think of.

Another very big shop had a very strange door on it: a tall, shiny thing which turned slowly around, with people going in and out of it. There was a *faint* smell of food in there, so he decided to investigate further, and waited for a space to come around before stepping inside. As he did so, the door-thing behind him swung and trapped his tail.

"YIP!"

He yelped and shot forward, hitting the door-thing in front. The door behind pushed him on and he found that he had to keep going. Round he went, picking up speed, faster and faster. He began to panic, barking furiously, and curious people began to gather. He felt his stomach begin to become agitated, and sure enough his system took over. The result was a long and very loud bottom *buuurrrrpp…!* Because of the rapid swinging of the door, to the people watching both on the pavement and in the shop, the sound was similar to the one you might get if you ripple a pack of cards.

The movement of the swing door wafted the niff out, with the result that all those waiting to enter, as well as all those waiting to leave the building, were introduced, first-hand, to the wonders of Ripley's rear end!

In no time, both the pavement and the shop foyer were strewn with coughing bodies, some unconscious. Others ran, staggered or crawled away, according to how badly they had been affected, while more than one person, safely distanced, could be seen waving alarmed hands and calling for help on their mobiles.

After about five minutes of this, Ripley began to tire, and so the door began slowing. Consequently, next time the exit to the street came around he leapt out, being careful not to trap his tail again, and rocketed up the road, where he found a fountain. He had a drink and a splash, shook himself dry over a couple of office girls and their sandwiches, then trotted on. As he did so, two of the *very* big things on wheels, the ones which had flashy-light things, swept by him in the direction he'd just come from.

Most of the other shops he came across either smelled of nothing much or of things that couldn't be eaten, and by this time he was starving.

Then, he rounded a corner and came across a shop *s-o-o-o-o* perfect that he just stood and stared at it, unable to believe his doggy eyes. Saliva ran like a river from his jaws, as he saw the dream of every dog in the world: it had meat of every possible kind!

*hanging meat…

*piled-up meat…

*meat in trays…

*meat on slabs…

and, *ooooh,* his fave!

*strings of fat, juicy, sausages…

He loved strings of sausages so much, because as soon as you ate one another came along, and another, on and on.

He crept up carefully and just stared at the sausages, his little mind trying to work out how he could creep in and snaffle one, without the feller in the striped apron and yellow (straw) hat – who looked angry to start with – seeing him.

Another big wheely thing, also with flashy lights and making a noise like *"nee-naw"*, shot past, toward the swingy-door place. Shoppers were now crowding the pavement, trying to catch a nosy glimpse of what was going on up the street, and Striped Apron Man wandered out of his shop to look as well.

As he did so, Ripley wandered in and... *whip-whoosh!* He grabbed a string of sausages, turned and belted down the street, as fast as he could. The butcher could do nothing but shout nasty threats, which he was very good at (he could easily have won a Nasty Threat Shouting Contest), and shake his fist at Ripley as he disappeared from view.

Meantime, back at number 1 Gladioli Street, the family had long since realized that Ripley was nowhere around, seen the open door and started searching the street and surrounding streets to find him.

Dad was just putting his coat on, to try searching further afield, when a knock came on the door. Standing on the path were two men in warehouse coats with *"PEST CONTROL"* written on the front. One of them had a long pole and attached to it, a hook through his collar, was Ripley.

"This your dog?" asked the man.

Thankfully, there were no charges against Ripley, just a warning to the family to keep him under control, which they said they certainly would do.

The rest of that week went without a hitch – apart from the fact that they had to put up with the aromatic results of the sausages!

After the next panic exit from the living room, Dad got them all together and said that he'd come to a decision: if a solution wasn't found to Ripley's problem, he was very much afraid that they may have to return him to Animal Rescue.

FIVE

Advice

THINGS DIDN'T GET better. In fact, things got worse.

Next door's cat died unexpectedly and in mysterious circumstances (it was found draped over the garden fence between the two houses); it looked like it was trying to escape something at the time, and had expired in the attempt. On top of that, the family panic exits from the living room were getting more frequent, and the pong was lingering longer.

The family seemed to have done everything that they could to combat Ripley's problem, and it began to look like they were doomed to spend the rest of their lives with a smelly, wilful, ever-hungry dog – one they loved. Dad said that he would, sadly, have to return him to the Animal Rescue people first thing on Monday.

But it was while Erin and Jacob had Ripley out on what was to be his very last walk, on Sunday, that a glimmer of hope seemed to present itself...

They took him on his fave run across the meadow behind the supermarket, then back through the streets leading up to the house. Ripley had been particularly "windy" that day, and they'd had to use the "smelly car fumes" excuse twice – once when they had run into schoolfriends, and then when 95-year-old Mrs. Fosby had stopped to stroke him. She was known to be a bit "whiffy" herself, so maybe she was used to "indelicate" aromas, but she did stagger a little, and blinked a lot as she trundled off, gripping, white-knuckled, to her Zimmer.

The problem was, now that Ripley was getting a bit bigger, his trumps were growing louder, and it was becoming a problem to pass people without getting a look of disgust. The kids were used to coughing loudly when this happened, to cover the sound, but today they were so sad that they didn't bother. One woman they passed was heard to say to her husband, in a sneery voice: "Humph! Children of today!"

They had stopped at an ice-cream shop to get a lolly each, and Ripley had plonked himself down just in the shop doorway. He decided to "perform" just as an elderly man in a raincoat came out, and walked right into it. He blinked a bit then smiled, took a deep breath through his nose and gave a satisfied: "Ahhhhhh!"

Jacob and Erin were just about to go into the "smelly car fumes" routine when the old man looked across at them wistfully, rolled his eyes to Heaven and said:

"Memories... Such memories."

Erin and Jacob exchanged a puzzled look. "Pardon?" said Jacob.

"Memories," repeated the old man. "I had a dog like that, once. 'Windybum' I called him... Loved him to bits." He wiped a little tear from his eye, as he bent and rubbed Ripley's ears. Ripley farted again in gratitude. The old man's next comment was a complete surprise:

"Bet you're looking for a way to stop him doing that, eh? Farting?"

"Well... we... err... we..." they stammered, both bewildered and embarrassed by the man's forthrightness, not to mention the state of his raincoat.

"Meat," said the old chap.

"Ermm... meat?" said Erin.

"Meat," continued the man; "don't give him none. Worked for me and Windybum. The day I stopped his meat ration was the day he did his last trump. Mark my words, it works."

Then he rubbed Ripley's ears again and shuffled off.

Back home, Mum was delighted to hear of their encounter, and immediately set about working out a feeding schedule for Ripley, which excluded anything with meat in it.

Dad was sceptical. "But you've only got the word of a man we haven't even met!" he groaned. "He could be... well... *anybody*!"

"You have any better ideas, Robert?" said Mum, acidly.

He hadn't, so he agreed to postpone Ripley's departure to the Animal Sanctuary for another week, until they had tried out the meatless diet.

Meanwhile, they decided they'd give the living room over to Ripley, and from the internet Dad bought a second-hand scuba-diver's oxygen tank and nose-pincher, which he hung in the hall; whoever's turn it was to feed Ripley had to wear it before going into the front room to feed him. They took it in turns to spend some time with him in there – all oxygened up, of course! The vet's super-duper surgical masks had long since stopped working; the elastic had perished.

Mum's menu for him turned out to consist of mainly three things: green beans, lentils and carrots. But, just to make it less "samey", she altered the proportions daily:

*Monday would be lots of green beans, with lentils and carrots…

*Tuesday would be lots of carrots, with lentils and beans…

and:

*Wednesday, she decided she would give him equal portions of lentils, carrots and green beans, with a lettuce leaf…

The rest of the week was a repeat of Monday, Tuesday and Wednesday, but on Sunday she threw in a roast spud. Jacob insisted he should have some tomato sauce on it, 'cos "everything tastes better with tomato sauce."

Well, not only did Ripley love his new diet, but the

problem lessened dramatically – not completely, but it gave the whole family hope that, after being fed like this for long enough, there was a chance that Ripley would, eventually, become a stink-free, normal dog-animal.

And it might have worked, except...

SIX

Chops

ONCE BACK ON his vegan diet, Ripley continued to improve, to the extent that the oxygen thing wasn't needed anymore, and the nose-clip thing was used only "in case".

It was about a month later that the travelling fairground came to the town, as it did every year, and set up in the local park. The kids always looked forward to it. Not only did it have rides that made you feel sick after a bellyful of candy floss, it had stalls where you could throw things and win prizes:

*hoops to throw around pegs…

*darts to throw at cards…

and:

*balls to throw at coconuts…

If they had wet sponges to throw at teachers, it would have been the world's most perfect place!

Ripley hadn't been out at all since the fairground took

over the park, and the kids managed to convince Mum and Dad to let them take him with them, pointing out that no dog should be expected to stay indoors 24/7. Dad got him a new lead, strong enough to stop a bull from running off, and they promised to keep him on that lead the whole time.

On the first day of the fair – a glorious day – they wandered around just breathing in the colours, seeing how much fun they could get out of their money and still have some left. They stood for a while outside the Palace of Oddities, wondering if it was worth paying to see the Three-Armed Woman, the Fabulous Monkey Man and the Elasticated Prince of Bendiland, but Jacob pointed out that there wasn't anything scary enough to see; certainly nothing as scary as the Wolfman they had seen last year. Milly reminded him that the "Wolfman" hadn't seemed half as scary when they had spotted him later, having a fag behind a caravan, with his fangs sticking out of his top pocket. They walked on, and it became apparent that Ripley was trying to pull-steer them toward the many fast-food trailers which dotted the park. But Milly, who had the lead, kept him away from them, knowing well what the results would be if he was able to get his teeth into a carelessly positioned beefburger.

Becoming tired of pushing through the crowds, they tried taking shortcuts through the ring of caravans which skirted the attractions. One caravan they passed had a sort of veranda, and on this veranda was a little, plump woman, happily cooking marinated pork chops on a grill thing – the smell of them made the kids' mouths water. You can imagine what it did for Ripley…!

He stood there, rooted to the spot, a river of saliva juices working overtime, with his eyes fixed firmly on the objects of his desire. No pulling of the lead could move him, so they had to lift him bodily, and carry him out of sight of the tempting spectacle. Once around the corner, out of range of the succulent aroma, he was back to normal, but Milly made a point of giving his lead an extra wrap around her wrist.

They came to one of their favourite stalls, grand and ornate: the one where you bought a number (or more than one, if you were daft enough) and watched as an illuminated horse and chariot spun around above the stall, and numbers flickered in a lit sequence on a number board. When the chariot stopped, so did the light, and if it stopped on the number you had bought, you won. Erin had won on this twice last year. She'd won a goldfish in a plastic bag, which had sadly slipped into Goldfish Heaven before she even got home, then a grotty Paddington Bear, which looked more like the Frankenstein monster than Paddington, and which gave her nightmares for a whole week, as it stared at her from the chair in the corner of her bedroom. They ended up nailing it to the garage door, to frighten off burglars. Still, even though the prizes were rubbish, it was exciting to see the numbered lights tick down toward the number you'd bought... and then – more often than not – either stop before the light hit yours or tick past it. That was when everybody but the winner would give a groan and rip their ticket up.

Today, the lights seemed to be travelling faster than usual, flashing hypnotically through the numbers, from one to a hundred *three times*, the chariot whizzing around before beginning to slow... slow... slow... until... *PING!* It stopped on number 39!

Milly's number!

She threw her arms up in delight.

Then her joy-filled face froze, as she realized that Ripley's lead was hanging loosely from her wrist!

This was unknown; he'd never done this before. Ripley had actually slipped his collar!

"Where is he?!" she cried, and the three of them swept their gaze around the immediate area. Nothing! Not a sight or sound of Ripley, nor any dog, anywhere!

The stallholder was still holding out her prize – another goldfish – but she ignored it. In a panting panic they extended the search, being careful not to lose sight of each other in the crowd. Where would he have gone? Somewhere with...?

"Food!" cried Erin.

Almost as one, they turned and raced back through the caravans, toward the spot where Ripley had been immobilized by the smell coming from the pan on the veranda.

They never reached the spot because there, charging toward them, a large, marinated chop in his jaws, was Ripley. Behind him, swaying dizzily on her veranda, was the plump, little woman who, only minutes ago, had been cooking it. As Ripley saw them, he darted down a gap to the left, and on into the swell of the fairground. They followed his bushy tail past the Swirling Teacups, twice around the Helter Skelter, through the chaos of the trampoline enclosure, to the far edge of the fairground, where the last attraction stood – the most ominous and spectacular, heart-jumping attraction of them all…

The Ghost Train!!!

Beyond that was open parkland.

A line of carriages carrying squealing, jittery, fright-hugging people was just about to take off into the Ghost Tunnel. Ripley looked like he was going to run past it and off into the park when, for some reason, he seemed to change his mind, swerved and leapt aboard the front carriage, which happened to be the only one empty (who would want to be the first in the queue to meet a ghost?). Before the kids could get there, the snake of carriages disappeared into the tunnel, and Jacob swore he heard a distant bark of joy as it went.

There was nothing they could do but wait until the train had completed its journey, and arrived from the other end of the tunnel, in… what… five minutes? Ten? Ever?

They looked up at the sign:

"THE WORLD'S SCARIEST GHOST TRAIN."

"Well," said Milly, "if it wasn't before..."

The others finished the sentence for her: "...it certainly is now!"

More and more people were gathering for the next trip, and by the time the train arrived, having completed the circuit, there must have been upward of fifty people eager to board. That all changed as the carriages exited the tunnel and rolled past them. Ripley sat regally in the front seat, a self-satisfied gleam in his eye and licking his greasy chops, while every carriage behind him was filled with unconscious people, spread in every possible position of recumbence. The waiting crowd took in the sight, backed away and dispersed, like fog in sunlight.

SEVEN

Pies

ONCE AGAIN, THE family had to endure the results of Ripley's naughtiness, though since the last incident Dad had installed an industrial-strength blower, which looked a bit like a jet engine but blew away the pong – and everything else in the room that wasn't tied down!

There was great excitement when it was announced that a Famous Television Personality was to visit the town, to open a new Very Big Pork Pie Factory. Jacob remarked that, in his opinion, a new pork pie factory was the very last thing that the world needed, for three reasons:

1. We can all easily live *without* pork pies…

2. The Famous Television Personality could put their time to better use, like opening a new Lego factory or a pet shop which sold real, live silverback gorillas… and:

3. Too many pork-pie factories would mean that the pig

could become the first domestic animal in the world to become an endangered species...

Mum decided that they should all go to see the ceremony.

At first, Jacob said, "No." But when he realized it meant a day off school, he said, "Yes!"

When they got there – what a crowd!

There couldn't have been more people there if they had expected to see Her Very Majesty the Queen playing keepy-uppy with David Beckham! Instead, a big, snazzy car drew up and out of it stepped the Famous Television Personality: none other than D.J. Billy Dripp, fresh from his appearance on T.V. swallowing a cupful of maggots.

Two people cheered. About a hundred turned around and went home.

The Town Mayor, along with the owner of the Very Big Pork Pie Factory (who looked like he'd been eating nothing but very big pork pies since he was three and, by the look of his teeth, had a dental problem), were there to greet him. The owner just about managed to stretch his arm over his own stomach to shake Billy's hand. As it was, he bowed so low that he caught his teeth on the top pocket of Billy Dripp's jacket and ripped it off. With so many people watching, Billy just laughed it off, but something about the way he grabbed the lapels of the factory owner's jacket, then kneed him in the crotch, suggested that he was less than happy.

As Billy and his glamorous girlfriend Petruliania (whose parents must have picked her name out of a Scrabble box) entered the Pork Pie Factory, a black, curly dog was seen by some to turn the corner of the building and trot in behind them. One of the some who saw it was Mum.

"That was Ripley!" she croaked.

"Eh?" said Dad, afraid to admit that it might have been. "Never saw a thing."

But Mum was convinced. She stood in Mum-thought for a moment, then said: "Robert, did you shut the kitchen window like I asked you to?"

"Of course, dear," he said. But his face told a different story: the story it told was, "I *think* I did."

Five minutes passed, and with nothing to look forward to, except seeing Billy Dripp again when he came out, people were beginning to drift away. Then there was a sudden commotion, as from the factory people came running. First the Mayor, with his Chain of Office hanging down his back and a wild look on his face, then the other dignitaries, pushing and pulling each other to get out faster, followed by the factory owner, his belly lurching like a balloon in the wind, his shirt hanging out. All of them seemed to be holding their noses.

Last to emerge was Billy Dripp himself, plaiting his legs as he went, walking slow and dazed, placing one foot carefully in front of the other as best he could. He didn't stop until he reached the door of his snazzy car where, out of habit, he turned and gave a little wave to his fan(s), then fell backward onto the rear seat. His girlfriend Petruliania tottered up on broken shoe-heels, heaved into the car and they were driven off, sharpish.

The crowd were open-mouthed, and hardly anybody saw the black, curly dog calmly trot from the factory, with a large bag of something clenched between his teeth.

Not a word was spoken on the way home.

Mum stormed inside and discovered that the kitchen

window *was* open, but also that Ripley was fast asleep in his basket.

"It couldn't have been him," said Milly, "that's exactly where we left him."

Mum walked over to the corner and picked up a torn paper bag. On it were the words: *"BRO S R IOUS P K PIE "* – all that was left of the label which had once read, *"BROWN'S SCRUMPTIOUS PORK PIES."* Her face was like a thundercloud, dark and threatening, and Dad was suddenly nowhere to be seen.

Ripley opened one eye, squinted and went back to sleep. The three kids *just* managed to keep from laughing until Mum stormed off, looking for Dad, then they laughed 'til they cried.

They had stopped laughing by the time breakfast came around the next morning – and a good job, too: the tiniest snigger from any of them could have ended up very badly indeed.

Mum warned them to keep a very close eye on Ripley, in an attempt to hide the fact that he belonged to them.

"As if a smelly dog wasn't bad enough," she hissed, "we

now have a dog that can manipulate people and use his...
his... *niffiness* to get what he wants!"

There was no doubt that Mum was mad, but the kids had
also no doubt that she loved Ripley as much as they did. She
was that kind of mum.

EIGHT

Change

ALL OF THIS was beginning to get Ripley's name known locally, and his antics, from time to time, would appear in print in the local paper. So, Erin had the idea to get some stickers printed, which said: *"FRIEND OF RIPLEY"*. It became quite the thing to be seen with one stuck on your jumper or coat.

It was Jacob who first pointed out that it was cruel to keep a dog confined to a room. "How about the shed?" offered Jacob. "To keep him in, I mean. It's a big shed."

"That's *my* shed," said Dad, sounding put out. "All my stuff's in there!" By "stuff" he meant his U.F.O. magazines, his spooky books, his star charts, his telescopes, his night goggles, his comfy armchair and his crate of beer.

"*MY* shed!" he repeated.

"Not anymore, Robert!" snorted Mum. "Jacob's right, it's a perfect solution. I want it cleared out by the weekend, please."

Dad's face fell, but he picked it up again, put it on and huffed. He was a particularly good huffer.

So, it was decided. The family would get their whole house back and the shed would become a huge kennel.

Milly, Erin and Jacob redesigned it and Dad, after seeing the sense in it all, reconstructed it. The door had a hanging pull-catch, which Ripley quickly learned to use, and a short rope on the inside of it, to drag it closed. There was a little window at Ripley height, and Milly made a curtain from one of Dad's old vests, which had its own gravy-stain pattern. When it was finished it looked lovely, like a huge doll's house, painted yellow with a sloping roof, and full of things to make Ripley happy. He just loved living in it, with the doors open so that he could have a good run and a frolic in the garden *(please look up the word "frolic"; it may not be what you think it is – Author)*.

In it, he had a little sleeping area, a heater, which they taught him to switch on when it was cold (though he never learnt how to switch it off) and an automatic doo-dah which, at the touch of a paw, would deliver food and water to his bowls. It also had rugs and a comfy chair for when visitors came to see him, which they sometimes did, just so that they could pick up their *"FRIEND OF RIPLEY"* sticker and make their friends jealous.

One regular visitor was Little John, who lived two streets away. Little John was a boy aged about fifteen, who they ironically called "Little" John because he was about seven feet tall (that's about two-and-a-half metres)! Just look now at the nearest door – go on, look! A normal door is about six-feet-six-inches high (about two metres), so that should give you an idea of how little Big John was... Erm... make that how *big...* erm... *Little* John was.

Little John was a boy with special needs and happy thoughts. With a smile a mile wide, he loved nothing better than to help people, and grew to love Ripley with a passion. And Ripley loved him back. He seemed immune to (what was left of) Ripley's pong and shared Ripley's garden time, even napping in the shed when Ripley felt like a lie-down. Little John came at least three times a week, more on sunny days, and the kids made him a *"Best Friend of Ripley"* certificate, which thrilled him to pieces. Little John's mum had it framed and he hung it on his bedroom wall. From then on, he insisted that any visitors to the house had to see it.

*

IT WAS DURING the time that Dad was converting the shed into a house for Ripley (and before he moved into the shed, this is), that Ripley turned from once smelly dog to superhero dog!

It happened like this…

NINE

Justice

WHILE THE FAMILY were sleeping one windy night – trees waving wildly, windows rattling – Ripley heard a noise at the back door and his ears shot up. He ran to the door of his room and sniffed at the gap beneath.

Strange, he thought, *nobody usually comes to feed me when it's this late and this dark.*

He thought this because food was *always* on his mind. But feet were quite definitely shuffling toward him, and he licked his chops in anticipation. If he'd had a napkin, he would have put it on and sat waiting.

There was no way he could have known that the house had just been broken into. But it had, by three men. Three men who had planned all of this very carefully. Robbers do that; they research their victims' houses to see what's what. They knew that in this particular house there was a dog, and that this dog had to be "taken care of" before anything else.

They were especially careful to do their research, after a robber friend of theirs broke into a house somewhere, without first checking if there were animals about, and the pet white rat which belonged to the boy who lived there ran up his trouser leg and bit his bum. He was caught by the police after a bum-examination of all the known robbers in the district (a job that police officers had to volunteer for). The teeth marks on his bum matched the teeth of the white rat exactly!

Ripley salivated as the door of his room opened just a crack, and a hand slid through. The hand was holding a small, juicy piece of meat, and whoever owned the hand tossed the morsel into the room, where Ripley devoured it with the speed of a starving shark. The door closed again and Ripley could hear whispering.

After a minute or two it opened once more, and a head, wearing a black balaclava with eyeholes, appeared. The head's eyes swept the room and rested on Ripley, tongue out, panting, eyes alert and a look on his face that said: "That was nice. Any more?" But the head withdrew and the door began to close.

Ripley, seeing his chance of a midnight snack disappearing, launched himself at the gap. He smelled the meat on the hand of the balaclava-wearing head and gripped its sleeve in his jaws, dragging the robber back into the room. The other two followed as quietly as they could, closed the door and tried frantically to free their friend, shushing each other as they did so and trying, at the same time, not to excite Ripley into barking. But Ripley hung on, the thought of another meaty snack spurring him on.

The tug-of-war must have lasted a minute, maybe two, when Ripley began to feel strangely sleepy. The strength began to fade from his jaws and his eyelids became heavy. The sleeve of his opponent suddenly slipped from his grasp and Ripley's head drooped. He swayed on his feet, then sank to the floor with a sigh. Silence fell, but the sound of it falling was broken by a light, rippling snore as Ripley slid into dreamland. The three robbers blew a sigh of relief (well, one sigh each, actually).

"More knockout juice next time, Kevin," whispered the biggest of the three, and Kevin nodded nervously.

"Right," said the big one, "we might as well do this

room first."

As quietly as possible they began to ransack the place, pulling out drawers and opening cupboards, ready to bag anything that looked remotely valuable.

Now, if they hadn't closed the room's door, they might have stood a chance. As it was...

It didn't take long for the drugged piece of meat to take effect on Ripley's stomach, reactivating all the dormant gases that his vegan diet had suppressed for months. The trump itself was a belter and could, with a little more force, have woken the family.

As it was, it startled the trio of robbers with its velocity, and each began to blame the other. They also did the worst thing they could have done under the circumstances: they each sucked in a breath, as one does when one is startled by a sudden noise. Horror immediately lit their faces and they clutched at their throats.

Kevin dropped first, totally unconscious, followed by the big one, clawing panic-stricken at his balaclava. The last one managed to stagger as far as the door on his knees, before collapsing in a heap, his shaking hand just failing to reach the door handle.

And that was where Dad found them the next morning, Ripley sitting on the chest of the big one, chewing on the balaclava which had belonged to the robber called Kevin. The police were called and the trio were carted away, just as they were beginning to recover, wondering where they were and what on Earth had happened.

TEN

First Contact

IT WAS AT breakfast time, three days later, when the knock came at the door. Dad went to answer it. He was away a couple of minutes, then came back with a sour face – his own.

"Who was it?" asked Mum.

"The press," said Dad, disgruntled; "the *Harbington Gazette*. They heard what happened and want to run a story on it."

"Great!" cried Erin. "We'll be in the news!"

"*Not* great!" replied Dad. "We *don't* want to become known as the owners of the world's smelliest dog!"

"But we *are* the owners of—" Jacob began, but Dad cut him off abruptly, and the conversation, like a puddle in the sun, dried up.

"Pass the toast, Mary."

But it is a well-known fact that newspaper reporters are

some of the most persistent beings on planet Earth, with the possible exception of wasps at a picnic, though wasps wouldn't come knocking on your door quite so often. An hour later there was *another* knock at the door.

Milly answered it and standing there, pencil behind his ear and notebook in hand, was a reporter from the *Daily Fib*, accompanied by another from the weekly magazine *Believe It Or Not!* (of which Dad was a big fan). They were fighting as the door opened because, as well as reporters being the most persistent beings that there have ever been, they would probably rather eat stale armadillo droppings than let another reporter get a story before they did.

They stopped squabbling, pretended they were friends and said they wanted to see Ripley, and take a photo of him. Then, as a late thought, they added: "Please." They then spat a stream of questions at Milly (and Jacob and Erin, who had joined her), which none of them could answer, because Dad had warned them not to:

"How old is Ripley?"

"How long has he been farting?"

"Why is he called Ripley?"

"Who taught him to fart?"

"Does he specialize in catching just burglars?"

Thankfully, Mum arrived from hanging out the washing. She slapped them with a wet sock and slammed the door, trapping the big toe of one of them, who howled like a sick camel and shouted a swear word of the very worst kind.

"You didn't tell them anything?" asked Mum.

"No."

"And they didn't see Ripley?"

"No, but—" said Erin.

"But nothing," answered Mum. "Dad wants as few people as possible to know about this!"

Milly and Jacob nodded in understanding, but Erin just looked angry. "Why?" she barked.

"Because!" shot Mum.

"I know, but *why*?" fumed Erin. 'I'm proud of what he did, catching those robbers! He should get some credit for it, or... or be given a big bone, or something!!"

"Erin!" shouted Mum, in exasperation. "Just leave it, okay?!" And she stalked off, a determined look on her face.

As we all know, mums with determined looks on their faces *do* stalk a lot and should be treated with great caution, so Erin said no more.

Milly and Jacob studied Erin's anger-red face for a moment, waiting for it to turn purple, then when it didn't they shrugged and walked off. Erin sat on the stairs, fists under her chin, and fumed for a whole minute and about nine seconds. Then she jumped to her feet, opened the door and strode outside, her mind made up.

Next morning, the story hit the headlines and Erin was in trouble. Mum and Dad weren't talking to her at breakfast.

Not so much for telling the reporters all they wanted to know (she had even given them a photo of Ripley, which they had fought over, and the one with the sore toe had won), but for doing something that her parents had told her not to. They do that, don't they, parents? They tell you not to do something that you desperately want to do, and it's dead frustrating. But sometimes we have to remember that they probably have really good reasons, *that you don't know about*, for telling you not to do it. Right? Right, carry on...

So anyway, Erin wasn't being spoken to, and frosty

faces soured breakfast – even the toast had burnt from lack of concentration. But brothers and sisters can be good at times like this.

"Everybody would have found out sooner or later," Milly nodded; "you can't keep secrets long around here."

"It'll be a nine-day wonder, Robert," chipped in Mum. "You'll see, this time next week it'll all be forgotten about."

But was it? Not on your life! Not on anybody's life! Not on the life of the most famous person in the world!

Mum's *"this time next week"* started with a phone call from a researcher from a regional T.V. news programme, who wanted to do a feature on *"Ripley, Robber-Catcher"*.

Well, by this time even Dad, his objections worn paper-thin, had given up on trying to pretend that it hadn't happened, and that they didn't own a dog of special interest (and very *special* habits). Besides, his fave magazine *Believe It Or Not!* had been in touch, and were interested in running a story.

ELEVEN

Exposure

THE INTERVIEW FOR the regional T.V. show, it was decided, was to be done "offline" and recorded, to be shown later. This, of course, was in case Ripley decided to live up to his reputation. But when Mum assured them that without meat he was as "safe as houses", they agreed to let the interview go out live. When Mum said "safe as houses", she must have been talking about *condemned* houses!

In the studio, Dad, Mum, Milly, Jacob and Erin, with Ripley, all sat on a long settee thing, while the girl who was hosting the show – the very glamorous Zoe Upshirt – sat facing them, behind a desk. There were cameras all around, getting views from different angles, with one directly on Ripley to catch his expressions. Twice before going live the sound technicians had to change the microphone cover, when Ripley licked it sticky, mistaking it for a black pudding.

Finally, it was "go!"

Zoe Upshirt glowed into the camera and introduced the family. "Take us through the story, stage by stage," gleamed Zoe, her twinkling eyes above a banana of a smile, framed by a hairstyle so elaborate that it wouldn't have looked out of place in a poodle parlour.

Dad took over, telling her, first of all, what a coincidence he thought it was that the robbers had actually used drugged meat on a dog whose diet precluded meat. "Strange, that, don't you think?" he mumbled. He would have gone on, but Mum sensed an attack of "mysterious happenings" from her husband and took over.

She got as far as the robbers drugging Ripley, when one of the cameramen began to cough... then splutter... then his knees melted and he sank elegantly to the ground, in a sitting position. Funnily enough, it was the cameraman nearest to Ripley.

Erin, on the end of the settee and also quite close to Ripley, but more accustomed to and therefore less affected by the Ripley niff, gave a groan and muttered: "Oh, no!"

Then another cameraman's groan overshadowed hers,

as he gave a lurch, staggered a bit and quietly vomited over Zoe Upshirt's hairdo. About the same time, the old familiar pong began to spread around the studio. Everyone vacated the space about as fast as one of those Japanese bullet trains!

Once everyone was in the corridor outside the studio, eyes streaming, they peered in at Ripley through the safety glass. He was sitting in Zoe's chair, looking straight into the camera, which was still transmitting, his tongue lolling, and obviously wondering why human beings have this habit of running from a room. Anybody viewing at home, who might have, say, left the room to make a cup of tea, would have come back in, seen Ripley and thought that Zoe had changed her hairstyle. Others who saw the whole thing said later that it was the best bit of telly they'd seen since... ever!

"Who gave him meat?!" Mum asked everyone, furious. Nobody had.

"Come on!" she shouted. "Somebody did! Who was it?"

"I gave him a biscuit," admitted Jacob.

"Biscuit?" said Dad. "What kind of biscuit?"

"Just, like, an ordinary biscuit… from his tin, before we

came out – the ones he always has," added Milly.

There was a silence, then the producer of the show – a lardy man called Boston; "Bossy" for short – raised an unusually timid hand.

"Erm… it… it might have been me," he stammered, knowing that this time next week he'd probably be stacking shelves at Tesco – if he was lucky.

"What?!" cried a gooey Zoe, with sick and bits of carrot dripping from her matted hair.

The producer looked sheepish (which is a very difficult thing to do unless you're a sheep). "So..." he stammered, "I… I was eating a sausage sandwich when you all came in…" He paused and gulped. "I dropped it and..."

He didn't get any further; Mum swung her handbag in a complete circle and caught him in the midriff. The sound his fat bottom made when this happened would have made even Ripley jealous.

TWELVE

Fame

WELL, *THAT* BIT of footage went viral!!

National newspapers, B.B.C. and I.T.V. news, foreign news programmes, YouTube, MyTube, TheirTube, cardboard tube and every other tube that existed showed it, and it had three trillion "likes" worldwide. It went straight to the top of every country's *T.V. Bloopers* show and, except for Eskimos in the frozen north and natives in the South American jungle, everybody on the planet must have seen it.

Suddenly, everybody wanted to know all about Ripley the Robber-Catcher.

At number 1 Gladioli Street, letters from all over the world began to pour through the Wigglesworth-Winterbottoms' letterbox, and the postman got a muscle rupture because his mailbag was so heavy. For weeks afterward their mail had to be delivered by van. Soon, tourist buses began to change their route so that they could crawl past the house and show their customers just where the famous Ripley lived. Some of the coaches stopped so that passengers could get off and photograph the house.

Milly, Jacob and Erin were kept very busy opening the mountain of letters and writing replies. None of them wrote the same reply twice. Sometimes it was:

* *"Thank you for your letter. Ripley was very pleased to receive it."*

Other times, it might be:

* *"Ripley woofed when I read it to him,"*

or:

* *"So good of you to write to Ripley, etc., etc."*

After a while, they began to get inventive and would write things like: *"A lick and a woof from Ripley,"* then add a smear of marmalade to represent the lick, but Mum spotted that one and told them they couldn't, because they were running low on marmalade. The cost of the postage was so much that Dad had to work extra hours at his horribly horrid job to pay for it.

The response was, in fact, so huge that it sparked an idea

amongst the kids.

"He's really famous," Milly mused. "He must be if he's getting all this fan mail!"

Erin brightened. "You're right!" she said. "Fan mail... Maybe we should start—"

Jacob finished the sentence: "A fan club?"

"The R.F.C.!"

"What? Reading Football Club?"

"The Ripley Fan Club!"

So it was decided and, with Mum's permission, they set about organizing it. They set up a template on the computer that prospective Ripley fans could use, then Milly downloaded a paw print as a kind of "pawtograph" from Ripley, as they worked out how to publicize the Fan Club and how to raise Ripley's profile (Ripley, of course, didn't even know he *had* a profile, *or* that it was about to be raised). They decided on a membership fee of one pound per month (outvoting the over-ambitious Jacob, who would have liked to have charged a hundred pounds a month!), then they chose Ripley's best photo – the one with his daft face and his tongue hanging out – and copied it about a thousand times. This used up six ink cartridges – Dad choked on his toast when he found out. Jacob said that they should have a dual photo, with his bum next to his face, since that's what he was famous for, but Mum banned that, too.

They spent all of the next Saturday sticking the copies anywhere they could (and some places where they couldn't) around town. Pretty soon, almost everywhere you looked you'd see Ripley looking back at you! They stuck them on:

*lamp-posts…

*shop windows…

*bus shelters…

*walls (double-sized copies)…

*factories (triple-sized)…

*supermarket trolleys (ribbon-sized, stuck on the handle)…

Milly even went to the graveyard and put some on the gravestones, because:

1) The place looked "dead" sad…

2) She knew the graves would have visitors…

and:

3) She thought that a happy, doggy face might cheer the

visitors up…

This worked, except for those grave visitors who had a doggy that had gone to Doggy Paradise – they sniffled.

Next, they decided to pool all of their pocket money (except for enough to buy tubes of Joosyfroots, which they all loved), and with this they managed to buy advertising space in a number of magazines, such as:

Pets Weekly…

Love Your Dog…

Fan Clubs Monthly…

and:

Doggy Doos Review…

They tried, but they could not find a magazine called *Dogfart Daily*, or they would've targeted that as well.

The response was much better than they expected, and in the first month they had attracted over 200 fans and admirers.

"Wait and see, once the word gets out there'll be dozens more," said Erin.

She was right: there *were* dozens more – *dozens* of dozens more!

It took all of their spare time to run the club. They emailed a newsletter each month, explaining what Ripley had been getting up to since the previous newsletter, with photos, doggy recipes, little doggy stories and doggy jokes, like:

What do you call a magic dog?

Answer: a Labracadabrador.

or:

Man: "I need a dog."

Pet-Shop Owner: "Yes, sir, what kind of demeanour (mood)?"

Man: "Well, I need a guard dog, so 'demeanour' the better!"

or:

What is a bulldog?

Answer: a greyhound that ran into a wall.

Some fans requested a clip of Ripley's hair, but if they had complied every time with that particular request, Ripley would have been bald in about a month.

Soon they had enough money to buy real metal badges with Ripley's face on them, and an inscription which read around the rim:

"A TRUMP A DAY KEEPS THE ROBBERS AWAY!"

Mum thought this up, and she sold them the rights for a Mum-kiss each; they in turn sold it to the Fan Club members for one pound.

In no time, they had enough money to allow Dad to stop working extra hours. He was so grateful that he took the whole family to the cinema, to see *101 Dalmatians*.

Meat-free Ripley seemed now to be the perfect pet, and (fingers crossed) it began to look as though he was going to stay that way.

THIRTEEN

Vegan

MUM GOT A phone call from someone she didn't know, who identified herself as Ms. Ida Crumb, President of the N.V.S. – the National Vegans' Society. Mum agreed to meet her for a coffee.

Once settled in the El Vito Coffee House, Ms. Crumb took a sip of her environmentally sourced, Colombian roast decaf, and a bite of her teacake with low-fat spread, and got right down to business.

She was full of admiration, she said, for the way that Ripley had made the leap from carnivore to vegan, and would be honoured if Mum would give permission for her to bring Ripley's story to members of her organization, at a meeting arranged for next week.

Mum supped from her mug of tea with six sugars, took a bite from her custard slice and asked where the meeting was to take place. She nearly *choked* on her custard slice when Ida Crumb said:

"Hyde Park. There'll be ten thousand people there."

"Oh!" said Mum, so taken aback that she dipped her nose in her custard. "What would we have to do?"

"Simply be there," said Ms. Crumb. "I just want to show that, if a dog can do it, so can we humans. It's *so* important for the environment."

Mum finished her custard slice, wiped her nose, thought about it, then rang Dad and the kids. None of them could see how it could do any harm, so she said okay.

In gratitude, Ms. Crumb paid for Mum's tea and custard slice, and bought her a jam doughnut, as well.

*

BACK HOME, JACOB was being stroppy. "We're not going to have to learn vegan, are we?" he moaned.

"It's not a language," explained Erin. "It makes you live longer, and it makes animals live longer 'cos we don't eat animals. Everybody should be a vegan."

That evening, Erin was regretting what she had said,

when she was served a lettuce leaf with a tomato balanced on it, as the rest of the family tucked into spicy meatballs.

*

THE DAY OF the Vegan Society meeting arrived, and the whole family turned up at 11:00 a.m., as they'd been asked to. Mum, Dad and Ripley were taken onto the speakers' platform, where Ida Crumb had been talking for over an hour already, striding about and waving her arms in a very dramatic fashion. The kids were given seats down by the side of the platform, where they could see what was going on.

It was a bit impressive. Thousands of people were there, and some had placards with various pro-vegan slogans, like:

* *"THE PLANET NEEDS VEGANS!"*

or:

* *"PLANT LIFE FOREVER!"*

Then there was:

* *"MEAT IS MURDER!"*

Jacob wondered about that one. He'd had spaghetti

Bolognese the night before last, and couldn't imagine it having been murdered before he got it.

Ida Crumb was now making it quite clear how good it was to be a vegan, and how easy it was to become one.

"No, it's not," mumbled Erin, thinking back to the meatballs she'd missed out on last week.

As they watched, Ida suddenly pointed to Ripley. "Here we have," she said, "a genuine biological carnivore. An animal born to eat meat. Born to tear the flesh off the bone, because he knows no other way." A groan of disbelief ran through the crowd.

Ripley saw her pointing at him and gave her a puzzled look, his head to one side. Next, she took a big beef rib from a bag and waved it in the air for all to see. Some people in the crowd actually cringed at the sight of it, others covered their eyes and, somewhere, someone gave a sob.

"This dog," continued Ida, "a *mere* dog, has, I kid you not, made the leap from carnivore to herbivore!"

The crowd, completely in her sway by now, gasped and *oooh*-ed. Seizing the moment, she stepped over to Ripley and, holding the rib by the little end, swung it back and forth in front of his eyes. Ripley's eyes swung with it and, though Ida crumb didn't seem to notice, he began to salivate. Dad tightened his hold on the lead. Striding back to the microphone, she held the rib aloft.

"If he can do it, so can we!! So can others!!"

People began cheering, and slowly a chant emerged, from 10,000 throats: *"MEAT IS MURDER! MEAT IS MURDER! MEAT IS MURDER!"* Over and over.

A second later, Ida staggered and nearly fell over as Ripley ran, used her hip as a stepping-stone and jumped high in the air, to reach the rib. As gracefully as a ballet dancer and, of course, in slow motion, he collected it from her grasp, landed on all fours, then sailed off the platform altogether, crawled underneath and began to gobble it down.

The crowd fell silent and Ida Crumb looked stunned.

Mum rose slowly, took Dad by the arm and left the stage. There was nothing more to be said. Ripley had just said it all.

FOURTEEN

Choccy

THE R.F.C. JUST grew and grew, though there were some would-be members who thought that they were applying to join the Rotten Fruit Club, for people who preferred to eat their bananas after they had turned black. Others thought they were joining the Red Flip-Flop Club, so that, as members of that club, they could call nasty names to anybody *not* wearing red flip-flops. and paint slogans on walls saying: *"Red Flip-Flops Rule, OK!"* There was even an application from one person who thought that if he joined the Rich Footballers' Club, he might just get himself invited to some of the parties that rich footballers go to. Some people, eh?

Mum then had the idea for a "Ripley Cake Competition", which called for each member of the Ripley Fan Club to bake a Ripley-themed cake, for Ripley himself to judge. The winner would get ten pounds, meet Ripley in person and would be allowed three strokes of his head – or four, for an extra ten pence.

Surprisingly, only one person entered, a girl by the name of Iolanthe Burp, who had bought a sticky doughnut, given it two buttons for eyes and sprinkled some hair, cut from her cat, on the top. It looked like exactly what it was: a hairy doughnut with scary eyes.

However, when, in order to attract more entrants, the prize for the best cake was raised to a hundred pounds, *un*surprisingly they got loads and loads of entries, from loads and loads of people. Most of the cakes were replicas of Ripley himself, and covered with either chocolate or black treacle, though one person had the idea of pouring black paint on theirs. Dad only discovered this *after* he'd sucked a finger full. One cake was shaped like a doggy bum, with a feather for a tail, and there were at least five cream-filled Ripley heads – down to three, after Ripley scoffed one and peed on another. It was much later that the family realized perhaps it would have been better if they had asked the members to send a photo of their cake, instead of sending the actual cake itself, because pretty soon the hallway was jammed with cakes of all sizes and descriptions, in tins, on tin lids, in boxes, cartons, wrappers… in fact, anything you could put a cake in or onto. One had been left on the doorstep, but had to be disqualified for having a big footprint in it. Nobody owned up to stepping in it, but two pints of milk on the step and chocolate footprints down to the gate told their own story.

Almost all of the cakes were made of chocolate, and the thought occurred to them that maybe they shouldn't have been tower-stacked quite so close to the radiator in the hall. When they all got up the next day, there had been a great melting overnight, which had covered the hall carpet in sticky, brown chocolate, strewn here and there with cardboard, tin lids and strawberry jam. Iolanthe Burp's doughnut was floating on the top like a lifebuoy. By lunchtime, the whole lot had set hard, due to a draught from underneath the front door.

They thought that the best way to clear it up would be to leave the front door open and put a sign by the front gate, saying:

"FREE CHOCOLATE – HELP YOURSELVES!"

A few people did, but the pieces that they ate tasted carpet-y, and the fluff got stuck in their teeth. One old lady's false teeth got stuck together in her mouth, and Dad had to use a screwdriver to lever them out. Word got around, and after a couple of days no one else came, so they had to hire a skip and shovel the lot into it.

Nobody won the hundred pounds.

FIFTEEN
Theatricalities

SOMEBODY (PROBABLY MILLY) pointed out that all fan clubs held conventions and meetings for their members, and that it might be a good idea to hold something that Ripley's fans could attend, to actually see him in person.

Jacob loved the idea, and said that it should be held at Manchester United's football stadium and opened by George Best, who he had been told was the best footballer the world had ever seen. It was left to Dad to break the news to him that:

*Manchester United would probably charge more than a million pounds to rent out their stadium…

*Ripley had probably only enough fans to fill three rows of seats…

and:

*Unfortunately, George Best had sadly passed away in 2005…

"Oh... right," said Jacob.

But the idea was a good one, they told him – just a little over-ambitious.

They managed to hire a small cinema in nearby Littlewick, sent out the invitations, then got down to organizing what should happen on the day.

Every member in the country attended and, as the day arrived, all 310 seats in the cinema were filled with people chanting, *"Rip-lee! Rip-lee!"* at the top of their voices. Almost all of them had brought some kind of dog food, and when Ripley made his appearance on stage, accompanied by Erin and Jacob, the adoring crowd (who had mostly brought packets of dry pellet dog food) threw handfuls, which delighted Ripley. But the fans threw it so hard that later Erin and Jacob's legs looked like they had the measles, and they had to rub on Aunt Polly's Cream for Dog Pellet Injuries, which smelled like bad breath.

They had decided on the idea of re-enacting the robbers' incident, to entertain the members. Milly, Erin and Jacob dressed up as the robbers, in striped jerseys and balaclavas, and played out the scene. Mum made the wind noises, like the weather had been on the night, by blowing into a microphone off-stage. When it came to Ripley doing what he had done to disable the crooks, she made the appropriate noise while Dad puffed green powder onto the stage, with a pair of old bellows. The three "robbers" fell down and the audience loved it. A few even shed a tear.

They followed this with a sing-song of doggy-type songs:

*Erin and Ripley had a tug-of-war with a tea towel, while everybody sang "Let it Go" from *Frozen*…

then:

*With Ripley on a stool, centre stage, and the words on the screen behind him, they all sang "I'd Do Anything" from the show *Oliver*…

then:

*"Happy Birthday to You" was sung (except they used the word "doggy-day" instead of "birthday")…

When all was over, and the family left the theatre by the stage door, there was a crowd waiting not only for Ripley's "pawtograph", but also for the autographs of the family themselves. They felt quite famous

SIXTEEN

Appreciation

EVERY YEAR, WITHOUT fail, the Harbington Association of Businesses organized a festival, consisting of a street parade with "floats" – displays mounted on a wheeled platform (usually a van or lorry, with balloons and bunting) – which all drove in line through the town, one behind the other, with the band of the Sea Cadets leading the way.

Every year was the same: the same businesses on the same floats, in the same order, starting at the same time, going through the same streets and ending in the same sandwich buffet, at the same town square. But this year it was to be slightly different. The phenomenon that was Ripley Wigglesworth-Winterbottom had brought so many visitors to the town, who had spent so much money *in* the town, that the Association had decided to honour him by giving him his own float to ride upon, which would bring up the rear of the parade and allow the townsfolk to show their appreciation of his efforts. He was to sit on a cardboard throne, wearing a cardboard crown on his head, and a banner reading:

"COMETH THE HOUR, COMETH THE DOG!"

The family thought about this, and though they were pleased that Ripley was being honoured, they drew a line at the cardboard crown, because:

1. It was bound to slip off...

and:

2. They didn't want Ripley to look daft...

As Dad said, poetically: "No dog with dignity would be seen dead with a cardboard crown upon its head."

They realized that somebody would have to be on the float with him, and they argued about which one of them would have the privilege. All of them had good reason to be his companion on the parade, and it was getting close to fisticuffs when Milly had a bright idea.

"What about Little John?"

"Perfect!" everybody agreed, with much nodding.

They all toddled off to Little John's house, taking Ripley

with them, and found him supping cocoa from his Ripley mug, flipping through his Ripley scrapbook, surrounded by photos on the walls of him and Ripley, and his pullover covered in *"FRIEND OF RIPLEY"* badges. His *"Best Friend of Ripley"* Certificate was no longer on his bedroom wall, but hanging in prime position, centrally over the fireplace. This boy knew the meaning of adoration!

Ripley immediately jumped on his knee and began licking his face, his rear end wagging like a metronome at high speed (that's Ripley's rear end, not Little John's).

After he'd calmed his excitement (that's Little John's excitement, not Ripley's), Mum explained to him what the parade was all about and how, this year, Ripley had been given a float of his own.

"Trouble is," she said, "someone has to be on the float with him, and we don't know who that should be. Any ideas?"

"You," said Little John.

"Can't," lied Mum.

"Dad?"

"Can't," said Dad.

"Milly?"

"Can't."

"Jacob and Erin?"

"Can't," said Jacob and Erin in harmony.

Little John shrugged and put on a sad face.

"You?" asked Mum.

"Can't," said Little John, playing along with what he now thought was a game.

"If I ask you nicely?" said Mum.

Little John thought about it, then, "Can't," he laughed.

Mum looked across at Little John's Mum, who smiled at her to keep going.

Mum gathered them all around her on the settee. "What if we *all* asked you to be Ripley's friend on his float in the parade?"

Little John looked across to his Mum, who nodded yes, and a huge grin spread across his face.

"That would be good," he said and hugged Ripley.

On the day of the parade, the streets on the parade route were packed, as they were every year, even though everybody knew exactly what they were going to see. The only new item this year was going to be Ripley's float – and they all wanted to see that. Ripley had put Harbington on the map for the first time since... well... since maps were first mapped!

Ripley took his seat on his throne, not knowing what this was all about, but not caring anyway: as long as he was with Little John, he knew that everything was alright. Little John sat behind him so that he didn't block anyone's view on the journey, wearing a sort of tall "Noddy Holder" hat with Ripley's photo on it, and holding his framed *"Best Friend of Ripley"* certificate close to his chest. He did this because his mum had told him that his heart was inside his chest. He knew that hearts meant love, so where else was he going to keep it?

There was a discordant blare of music from the Sea Cadet band at the front of the line, then they struck up a marching tune. The parade moved off.

First came the float of Grave's Funeral Parlour, on which was a coffin and a tombstone, and a banner reading:

"WHEN THE TIME COMES, DIE HAPPY WITH US."

Two mannequins in black suits, tied to the back of the

float, pitched and swayed as the float moved along over cobbles. They hadn't gone five metres when one of them lost its head, which rolled into the crowd, where it was used as a football.

Behind this came C. Ment the Builder, with two fellers in impossibly immaculate overalls, holding up a brick each in one hand and a trowel in the other, against a background of brick wallpaper. Their banner read:

"LET US BUILD YOUR DREAM HOME."

There was a big picture of a home with manicured gardens, lawns, a tennis court and a swimming pool, which nobody in Harbington would ever have a snowflake in Hell's chance of buying.

Next followed the float of Willie Pullit, the dentist. He had a happy, jovial "patient" lying in his dentist's chair, a carefree grin on his face, while Willie pretended to be extracting a tooth. Every so often, both Willie and the patient would turn and wave merrily to the crowd, to show what a splendid time can be had at the dentist's surgery. The banner along the side of the float read:

"WE PULL THE TOOTH, THE WHOLE TOOTH AND

NOTHING BUT THE TOOTH."

And so it continued, with the Butcher *("100 YEARS OF 'MEATING' THE PEOPLE OF HARBINGTON")*; the Pickle Factory *("BE SURE TO HAVE A PICKLE EVERY DAY")*; and Bob Bunn the Baker, who blasted the crowd with a snowstorm of crushed bread from a blower, whilst shouting: "Crumbs!" Six months on, people would be finding crumbs in their clothing, their hats, their shoes and places you wouldn't expect a crumb to have gotten. The only winners were the pigeons, who swarmed in after the parade was over.

Everything was going well, with the crowd cheering and jeering as the floats went past – and not forgetting, as usual, to *boooo!* as the float carrying the Mayor and members of the Town Council went past. Some of the naughtier onlookers always threw tomatoes. This year, someone got *very* naughty and threw a half-eaten cheeseburger, which knocked the Mayoress's hat off and splattered everyone else on the float with pickle, onion, jalapenos and tomato sauce! A splodge of tomato sauce flew through the air and landed on Ripley's head, on the float behind. Little John was so annoyed, he shouted: "Oi!" He laid his certificate aside, took out his handkerchief and wiped it off of Ripley.

The cheers for Ripley as he went by were deafening, and Little John picked up Ripley's paw and waved it back. Then, grinning with delight, he gave Ripley his paw back and reached for his beloved certificate.

It wasn't there!

It wasn't where he'd put it, and alarm lit his face. Frantic, he looked under the seat. Finding nothing there, he panicked and searched every inch of the float.

"*Oh-h-h-h!*" he wailed, mortified at the loss.

Something caught his eye on the road behind them, and his wail became a shriek. Ripley eyed him anxiously, instinct telling him that something was wrong, without telling him what. The framed certificate was now lying in the road behind them, its glass cracked from the fall and cars passing over it, their wheels on either side.

Little John didn't hesitate; he jumped from the float, fell, picked himself up and made a beeline for it. Ripley took his cue from Little John and jumped off as well, yapping. Some canny individuals in the crowd ran also, anxious to be the ones who would be able to say that they'd actually been present at a Ripley incident – whatever it might turn out to be!

Minutes earlier, Ripley's float – the last in line – had just turned a corner, and right now vehicles were coming around that corner, some of them unaware that the parade was even there. But, at this moment Little John's sole thought was for the safety of his prized possession; nothing else mattered. Three more cars passed, straddling the certificate, while he hopped from foot to foot, awaiting his chance to grab it. Seeing a space, he ran forward, picked it up and hugged it to his chest, with a smile of relief. He was totally unaware that a fruit lorry had just rounded the corner, faster than it should have done, and was screeching its brakes as it slid, wheel-locked, toward him.

A second before it should have struck him, Ripley jumped and thumped him in the chest, knocking him to the side of the road, Little John losing a single shoe to the lorry's mudguard.

Whilst he was still in mid-air, the front grill of the lorry caught Ripley a thudding blow and he was thrown onto the pavement, where he lay motionless.

SEVENTEEN

Concern

THE FAMILY HAD been waiting with the crowd at the Town Hall Square, to see Ripley's float arrive. Then his float did arrive – empty!

The driver hadn't even noticed that his passengers had gone, 'cos he was scoffing a cheese pasty and waving to his mates when the incident had happened. He was as surprised as everyone else, when it was quietly pointed out to him that he was carrying an empty throne.

Quickly, anxiously, the family made their way back down the parade route, picking up bits of information as they went. Naturally, the further away from the happening they were, the less reliable the information was:

"Ripley ran off..."

"Ripley bit Little John, *then* ran off..."

"Somebody threw him meat..."

Then came:

"…some sort of accident, I think…"

and:

"…run over…"

That gave them wings!

They arrived at the spot, forced their way through the shoal of people, then stopped dead, mouths open. Ripley was lying where the lorry had thrown him and Little John was crouched over him, sobbing. They went over to him and he tried to push them away, until he recognized them – then his relief was something else.

"What happened?" Dad asked to anybody who was there.

Everybody tried to tell him at once – it was like having three radios on at the same time. But, through the well-meant babble, one word kept being repeated, and that word was: "Hero."

And that was the word that all the local (and national) newspapers used in their reports the next morning:

The Daily Posh: "HERO DOG SAVES YOUTH."

The Daily Fib: "RIPLEY THE ROBBER-STOPPER NOW HERO OF TRAFFIC ACCIDENT."

*

IN ALL, IT took two months for him to recover, and to become something like his old self again, but it was the busiest two months that the Wigglesworth-Winterbottoms had ever spent.

Considering that he'd bounced off the front of a speeding lorry, his injuries were not as severe as they might have been – though two broken ribs and a deep cut on his head were nothing to laugh about. The vet treated the cut but "ribs heal themselves" he told the family, adding, "He'll be sore for some time."

Once again, his fame spread like jam on a sandwich, and his Fan Club topped a thousand, when two families from China applied to join. Every fan already on the books either rang, wrote, emailed, texted, twittered, squeaked or messaged, wanting to hear at source everything that the newspapers and telly-casts had already told them. Flowers arrived by the hour, making the front room look like a botanical garden, and the number of people who knocked at the door, just to ask how he was, just couldn't be believed. Mum had to post bulletins on the front gate – in big letters for the short-sighted – charting his progress as he recuperated, but people kept stealing them as souvenirs.

Camera units set up outside and earnest, frowny-faced reporters spoke into the cameras, ending each report with: "This is Dolly Daydream (or whoever), News at four-thirty (or whenever), Harbington."

Poor Ripley. He could only creep about slowly for a month.

He got so many visitors that they ran out of *"FRIEND OF RIPLEY"* stickers in the first week. Little John had put himself in charge of visitors, and had to ask those who didn't get a sticker for their addresses, so that when the new stickers arrived he could deliver them. And he did, every single one, even though some lived out as far as Littlewick.

Such was the public interest in Ripley that a very well-known greetings card company offered to turn out postcards of him for visitors to the town to buy – like visitors to London buy postcards of Big Ben.

EIGHTEEN

Police

IT WASN'T LONG after Ripley's full recovery that the family found the police at their door. Well, "found" might not be the right word; they opened the door when the knock came and there they were. Or rather, there *he* was: a police inspector.

First, panicky thoughts were centred on, such as:

*had the T.V. studios or Zoe Upshirt complained and now wanted compensation?

or:

*did the T.V. producer who Mum had clobbered with her bag want her arrested for assault?

But no, he had come for a completely different reason.

Usually, inspectors do nothing but inspect, then tell somebody else what it is they want them to do, so the fact that this inspector had come himself was an indication, in their minds at least, of how important the matter was. He was tall and thin, and a little stooped. His name, he said, was Lector, which made him Inspector Lector. Jacob thought what a good job it was that he wasn't:

*a Plumber called Bummer...

*a Brickie called Dicky...

or even:

*a Fitter called Titter...

Anyway, Inspector Lector sat down and took off his inspector's hat. Straight away Dad had to turn the light off, because the reflection from the inspector's baldy head blinded everybody in the room. He also had a bushy moustache, which looked like a furry caterpillar was crawling over his top lip, as well as eyebrows which kept doing somersaults as he talked.

"I have come, Mr. and Mrs. Wigglesworth-Winterbottom *(eyebrows up)* with a business proposal." He sat back, one eyebrow twitching, and allowed his words to sink in.

"Err... what kind of... ermm... business proposal?" asked Dad, in his favourite and well-practised, most-suspicious-sounding voice.

"One which I hope will interest you," said Inspector Lector *(eyebrows up and down)*, and took a sip of the tea that Mum had made for him, eyeing the Jammy Dodgers she had put out on a plate.

"Do tell us more," said Mum.

The inspector dunked a Jammy Dodger into his tea, but left it in too long and it dropped onto the carpet before he could get it to his mouth. He didn't seem to notice this which, for an inspector, is a worrying sign. However, Ripley noticed and scoffed it quick. The Jammy Dodgers, it would turn out, were a bad move because, unknown to anybody, Inspector Lector was secretly addicted to them (much more about that later).

"We in the Police Force," went on the inspector, "are fortunate to have a division of very intelligent dogs to assist us *(eyebrows up)* when circumstances call for it."

"That's nice," said Dad, trying his best – but failing, as yet – to find something strange about all this.

"Yes," said Lector *(one eyebrow up, one down)*, "they can apprehend criminals, sniff out drugs, run really fast, scare people who need scaring and… err… all that sort of stuff."

The kids exchanged looks. Where was all this going? And were his eyebrows battery-powered?!

"What we don't have yet," he continued, "is a dog who, if trained to do so, can bring a hostage situation to an end *(just one eyebrow)* without actual loss of life."

"That would take a very clever dog," said Mum, politely.

"It would, indeed," said Inspector Lector (here, he looked at Ripley), "*or* one that had its own inbuilt disabling system."

He sat back again, eyes on the Jammy Dodgers, and there was a pause while the family took this in.

"You mean our Ripley?" gasped Milly.

The inspector spread his hands *(eyebrows up)* and shrugged, then reached for the biscuit plate. Ripley moved closer to him, remembering what had happened to the last Jammy Dodger this man had handled.

"No way!" blurted Jacob. "That's dangerous!"

Lector's eyebrows took a dive, and he looked suddenly very wise.

"Life itself is dangerous, son, but where there is danger there is excitement." He stretched his Jammy Dodger toward his cup, but thought better of it and popped it, whole, into his mouth. Ripley huffed and lay down.

"I don't think we'd be interested in that, Inspector," said Mum. "Besides, he no longer suffers from his digestive problem."

Lector did the eyebrow thing again and pushed his case. "But he could regain his… err… his skill, if his diet allowed it. Am I correct?"

"Out of the question," replied Mum.

Lector tried to reply through a mouthful of Jammy Dodger; it came out as, "Phut oo adent erd niovver yep!" along with a shower of biscuit crumbs. Ripley managed to vacuum them up almost before they touched the floor.

What that was *supposed* to sound like was: "But you haven't heard my offer yet!"

Then he swallowed the rest of the biscuit, coughed until he got a snotty nose, wiped it all over his moustache and said:

"One thousand pounds per month."

It was now time for Dad's eyebrows to shoot up.

"Very generous, Inspector," he said. "When would—?"

"But, as I said," broke in Mum, "we wouldn't be interested."

The inspector put on a look of deep disappointment which, given his snotty moustache, looked more like he had wind. He sniffed, stood up and, as the crumbs cascaded from his uniform (to Ripley's delight), he produced a business card from his pocket and handed it to Dad.

"If you change your mind," he said, "call me." And, with eyebrows perfectly level, he rose and turned to leave.

He then stopped, turned back and, with a mumbled, "You don't mind, do you?" grabbed a fistful of Jammies and stuffed them in his pocket. Then, with his baldy head held high and jam stains all over his tunic, he left as quickly as dignity would allow.

NINETEEN

Sand

EVERYBODY AGREED, WITH the exception of Erin, that they had made the right decision over Inspector Lector's offer.

Erin had thought that it might be something that Ripley would like to do, but when she heard that he would have to stay in police kennels all week, and only come home at weekends, she changed her mind.

With great difficulty, Dad put the thought of £1,000 a month, and what it might buy, to the back of his mind, and agreed as well.

A week later, there was a real-life hostage situation reported in all the newspapers. The person who had been kidnapped wasn't hurt, but she had spent two whole, horrible days locked in a room, and it made the family feel guilty, 'cos, if Ripley had been there he may have saved her more quickly. Still, their decision had been made.

Besides, Ripley had made such good progress with his diet – with only one minor setback, when he had snaffled a morsel of bacon off the kitchen worktop, and put the pet hamster to sleep with the results.

*

MILLY WAS A whole three years older than the twins, which made her nearly sixteen. She had two good friends, Rachel and Farrah, and the three of them shared everything, though Milly had tried to keep Ripley's problem from them for as long as she could, too embarrassed to explain. I mean, can you imagine it?

"Hi, Rachel... hi, Farrah. Did I mention that our dog farts all the time and the smell's terrible?"

You just wouldn't, would you?

But now, of course, with all the publicity, Rachel and Farrah knew all about Ripley, and that he was now all but cured (fingers crossed).

This particular day – a bright, sunny, let's-go-somewhere day – Milly found that she was the only one in the family able to look after Ripley, on the very day that she had planned to go to the beach with her two best friends. She was not over the moon about this at all. But Mum had a meeting to plan next term's school menu (Milly wanted to know why, since the same things were on the school menu each term, and had been since she had been in infants' class), Dad had to take the twins to the dentist (and then work late, to make up the time he'd lost doing it), and Ripley couldn't be left alone all day, in case his diet turned out to have unexpected and much-delayed side effects. So, Milly found that she had no alternative but to take him to the beach with her.

She took his food, some water, a battery-powered fan and half a dozen supermarket bags, just in case any late side effects *did* occur. Rachel and Farrah were happy to see Ripley, but Milly secretly hope that she'd still have friends by the end of the day – then convinced herself she was over-reacting. The beach was busy; happy people doing happy things, seagulls yodelling, waves lapping. But Milly (again, just in case) picked a quieter spot by the esplanade wall.

Now, for some reason that we will never know, as soon

as Ripley, for the first time in his life, felt the soft, warm sand between his toes, he reacted with an excitement something like that which Neil Armstrong must have felt when he stepped onto the moon.

"One small step for dog, one giant leap for dogkind!"

It sort of electrified him, and he leapt around like a wild horse at a rodeo. This was a clue – though the girls didn't spot it – to the fact that, by the end of the morning, he would become a big, black, curly, grinning, floppy, goofy, tail-swinging, tongue-lolling MENACE!

First, he tore along the waterline and back about a hundred times, without stopping, scattering paddlers and ankle-waders. Then he returned to the girls, stood panting and shook himself dry all over them. He then turned and shook himself even drier, over an elderly couple nearby. Apologies were futile and they shuffled off, disgruntled (which is worse than "gruntled"). He dug holes wherever he found space to dig them, throwing sand in every direction and ignoring the buckets, spades and flip-flops that people threw at him to make him stop. Then he played "destroy the castles", and kiddies up and down the beach wailed and cried as Ripley ran around, knocking down their carefully constructed sand creations and jumping on them, stiff-legged. Next (never having seen one before), he was delighted when he attacked inflatable monsters in the shape of beds and balls, which popped and died with one bite. He couldn't get enough of *them*!

Mothers began to gather their children and move off the beach altogether. One grabbed a convenient policeman and pointed Ripley out, as he was peeing on the head of a man who had been buried up to his neck by his children. She also pointed out Milly and her friends, who had been trying to make themselves as small as possible whilst all this was going on.

The policeman took strides toward them. It was obvious that he had come top of his training class in "striding", and now it was just as obvious that he was going to show Milly and her friends his "scowling" skills. By this time, Ripley (who now was looking more like a spiky, sand-covered, black bin-bag than a dog) had sniffed out and located a fast-food van, and now he stood salivating in front of it, his tongue almost to the floor. The policeman towered, scowling fiercely over Milly, Rachel and Farrah.

"There's been a complaint," he said, with a voice to match the scowl.

Milly nearly died of shame, and hurried to tell him how well-behaved Ripley normally was.   But he wasn't interested, and told them that they would have to remove Ripley from the vicinity at once, or be arrested for disturbing the peace and being in charge of a disorderly animal.

As he strode off, Milly turned in time to see Ripley wolfing down a huge bratwurst sausage, which had just slipped out of its bun while its owner was squeezing a ton of mustard on it.

"Ripley! Noooo!!" shouted Milly.

Startled, Ripley gulped and swallowed the whole sausage, mustard and all. He coughed, as mustard hit the back of his throat like a splash of lava. His eyes bulged, his tail shot up, straight as an arrow, and he looked around, desperately for water. He saw only the sea. Next minute, he was belly-deep in it, slurping. The saltiness made him gag and he spat out as much as he could, gasped and coughed again.

Then, a sort of dreamy, vacant look came over his face. It was probably a combination of sausage, mustard-shock and seawater that made him do it, but suddenly the water boiled around him, as he produced his first bottom-burp for months – his first-ever underwater one – and it was a monster!

The water boiled and, as it calmed, up from the depths floated fish, stunned and gasping. A minute later came up a guy in full scuba gear, his visor all foggy. He raised a weak arm then rolled over on his back, scuba tube pointing to the sky. Steam came from the sea around Ripley. The pong was diluted by the seawater, but as it crept ashore, like a pale green mist, hundreds of dazed crabs crept with it, each with one claw pinched around what must be their equivalent of our nose.

Ripley ran to Milly and lay on his back, while she poured down his throat all six bottles of water she had brought, followed by three bottles of cola she had packed for her and her friends.

It was a measure of what good friends Rachel and Farrah

were, that they took the whole incident in good part, and promised on Ed Sheeran's life not to say anything to anybody. Milly didn't mention it to the family when she got home, either.

Then, the local paper came out the next day, with the headline:

"MAD DOG CAUSES HAVOC ON BEACH!"

She hid it and told Dad it hadn't been delivered.

"Strange that," said Dad. "First time ever!"

TWENTY

Pencils

JUST A WEEK after the beach incident, something happened that changed everything: Dad lost his horrible job.

He was half relieved and half anxious, since his wages were important in keeping his family safe and fed.

It happened like this:

Apart from being *horribly* horrible, his boss was horribly grumpy, horribly mean, and had *extra* horribly horrid breath when he bent over to tell you off. Even his appearance was horrible. He was short and had a black moustache, just the width of his horrible nostrils; his hair was all slicked down to one side. He was called Littler – Ian Littler, actually – and had his name, in gold letters, on his office door: *"I. LITTLER"*. He wore boots with false heels, to make him look taller, and these boots "clacked" on the floor, so his staff could always hear him walking about – *clack-clack, clack-clack...* – all day long. He wore a khaki-coloured safari jacket which was about ninety years old, with a pocket on the chest, where he kept a little notebook to write in things that his staff did wrong.

Everybody there worked at separate desks in the same room, and had to be not just on time in the morning, but *early*. And, he didn't pay them if you had to work late, to finish what they were doing. At eleven o'clock, every morning (sometimes as late as two minutes past eleven), he'd step out of his office and blow a whistle. His office workers would scramble for the flasks of tea they had brought, and try to drink a cup before he stepped out again at exactly – *exactly* – five past eleven, blowing his whistle again. Lunch was a miserly half-hour, and nobody was allowed to leave their chair to eat.

The way he sacked Dad was particularly horrible.

Dad's pencil had fallen onto the floor, and Mr. Littler clacked over, picked it up and said:

"Pencil on the floor, Wigglebottom?" (He couldn't even be bothered to say Wigglesworth-Winterbottom).

"Sorry," said Dad.

"Don't let it happen again!" snapped Littler, and clacked

off.

But it was Dad's *own* pencil – Littler didn't supply any – and on this particularly fed-up day, particularly fed-up Dad thought: *I should be able to decide what I do with my own pencils, surely!*

So, the next time he heard Littler's boots approaching, he purposely nudged the pencil onto the floor again.

Littler stopped by Dad's desk, his face like a burnt crumpet, and swivelled his gaze from the pencil to the desk, then back again, three times. Then...

"Pick it up, Wigglebottom," he sneered.

Dad carried on working.

"I said—" began Littler.

"Pick it up yourself," said Dad, calmly.

Littler's mouth shrank as small as a cat's bum. He breathed deeply through his nose, and his eyes began to water from being squeezed almost shut

"It's *my* pencil," continued Dad. "I'll pick it up when *I* want to."

All the other staff were watching now, mouths open. Littler's face went pale as all the blood drained to his feet, then red as it all rushed back again. He broke out in a sweat and his hand shook, as he wagged a finger in Dad's face and stuttered.

"Is there something you're trying to say, Mr. Littler?" asked Dad, knowing that in about a minute he'd have no job. But right now he didn't care. He'd had enough.

Littler was in such a rage that he struggled to get the words out:

"Y... you... you..."

"Yes?" asked Dad.

And Littler very nearly exploded on the spot.

"Y... y... you're f... f... f... *FIRED!!*"

There was silence, except for Littler panting.

Then, into the silence crept a certain sound...

It was the sound of pencils dropping – *clink, clink, clink* – as, one by one, the rest of the staff shoved their own pencils off the edge of their desk, in support of Dad's brave action.

Littler looked around, his chest heaving in humiliation, then ran for his office, his boots going *clack-clackity-clack.*

So it was that, from then on, Littler had to treat his staff with a little more respect, knowing that if he sacked them all for dropping pencils, he'd have no workers, and no workers meant no business.

Later, to "save face" (though he didn't have a face that was worth saving), Littler reluctantly tried to give Dad his job back, but Dad really had had enough. He got a round of applause when he left.

But before he did so, he crept into Littler's office, while Littler was in the toilet, and nailed a big piece of fish – which was at least a week past its sell-by date – to the underside of his desk (*DO NOT TRY THIS YOURSELF!*). He heard, much later, that Mr. Littler didn't discover where the smell was coming from until the fish was at least a year past its sell-by date, and the room was full of flies.

TWENTY-ONE

Desperation

SO NOW, WITH only Mum's wage coming into the house, things were much tighter moneywise, and the family were in trouble. Everybody had to "tighten their belts" (except for Ripley, who didn't wear one).

*Breakfasts were limited to one Weetybisk a day...

*Joosyfruits became a distant memory...

*Toilets were only flushed twice a day, to reduce the water bill...

*Trips to the movies disappeared...

and:

*Telly got switched off at 7.30, to save on electricity...

Before long, they could barely hear themselves speak for the rumbling of their tummies, and it was decided that they needed the £1000 per month that Inspector Lector had offered them. So, they rang him and he came.

He ate seven Jammy Dodgers (three dunked), and

agreed to accept Ripley into the Police Force Dog Section the following week.

Erin cried and Jacob sulked. Dad said that as soon as he could get a new job, Ripley could leave the Police Force, but he couldn't say when that was going to be, and neither could Mum.

He really did try to get a new job, but he wanted one that he liked doing. If he could have found someone to employ him as a Paranormal Investigator, working for two hours a day with all meals paid for, on a wage of one hundred pounds an hour, and a chauffeur to take him to and from the office, then he would have taken it – but the Job Centre had none of that kind of jobs listed. The nearest thing to it was a vacancy for a sweeper-up in a spiritualist church.

Ripley, of course, had to share in the family's temporary hardship, except that he didn't know the reason they were all "hard-up". He did wonder why he was getting one lettuce leaf less in his bowl, and why the doo-dah in his shed was dispensing one scoop of beans instead of two. His squirt of tomato sauce only appeared every other day, as well.

What's going on here? he thought.

As a result, he tried very hard to find more food for himself.

The lock was still on the fridge door, so he couldn't paw that open, though he did try to bite it off, with no success. He began hanging around the dining table at mealtimes, but there was a family rule not to feed him at the table so, apart from the odd dropped potato, nothing. He tried the kitchen bin, but swing lids weren't his thing; no sooner had he nosed it open than the other leaf of the lid would smack him on the head.

But, Ripley had been through enough difficult situations to allow a bin lid to defeat him. He gave a Ripley-sized launch, got his head in, smelled food and thrust farther.

The lid won. It trapped his head in a bin's equivalent of a W.W.F. death-hold, and it hung on until Riley managed to jerk his head back.

Suddenly, he was staring at a decapitated bin – one with food in that he couldn't reach. And now, because of the bin's death-hold, he couldn't see a thing, and the whole kitchen began to attack him. Cups smashed at his feet, the toaster jumped on his back, a chair fell over and tried its best to trip him, and the plug lead from the microwave wrapped itself around his legs. The microwave itself launched itself onto his rear end, trapping his tail on the floor. He ran to where he knew the door was, but it had moved and he clanged into a radiator, instead. When the kettle joined in the assault, drenching him with water, he barked for help.

Help arrived in the shape of Milly, who used her cross/angry voice and tugged the lid off. The lid gave one last bite to his ear, then the world appeared again, as if by magic. The door had returned to the place it should be, so he flew through it, skidded on the carpet and hid behind the T.V.

That night, with everybody in bed, there came a dull thud from somewhere outside, which was loud enough to wake them all up (except Jacob, who doesn't even wake up for his morning alarm, and would cheerfully sleep through an earthquake). Individually, everyone blamed something different for the noise: Erin thought it was the wind; Milly blamed a cat; Mum thought it was a car door being slammed; and Dad just *knew* it was a small meteorite hitting the ground.

But, eventually they all dropped off to sleep again.

Minutes later came a scraping sound: *scrape*-(pause)-*scrape*-(pause)-*scrape*...

Dad, Mum, Erin and Milly all arrived on the landing at the same time – Dad with a flashlight and a Klingon/English dictionary – and the four of them tiptoed down the stairs, through the kitchen and out into the back garden. Dad switched on the flashlight, all ready to hold up a V-shaped hand and proclaim: "We mean you no harm."

What they saw was the wheelie bin, upside down, wheels in the air, inching its way along the concrete path – *scrape*-(pause)-*scrape*-(pause)-*scrape* – leaving a trail of rubbish in its wake. Dad was overjoyed – this could be the first sighting of a spiritually-possessed wheelie bin ever recorded.

Except for one thing: a black, bushy tail sticking out from underneath the bin's edge. Neither would a wheelie bin, possessed or not, have answered to the shout, "RIPLEY!!" before giving a jump and toppling over.

Something had to be done. No family should have to

live like this! Dad *had* to find a job, whether he liked the job or not.

He tried harder, and these are just some of the jobs he managed to get:

*Crab-catcher for a seafood restaurant (he retired with pinched-finger syndrome)…

*Naked artists' model (nobody could paint for laughing)…

*Office pencil sharpener (he just didn't get the point)…

*Cat-chaser, for a dog too fat to run (so was Dad)…

*Wringer-out out of wash leathers, for a one-armed window cleaner…

And:

*Coffin-carrier (he found this *dead* boring)…

He even got his old ukulele out from under the bed, dusted it off, sandpapered the rust from the strings and stood outside Marks and Spencer's, with his cap on the ground, and busked. It didn't go very well, mainly because all that he could play was one *"plink"* followed by two *"plonks"*, and *"plink-plonk-plonk"* didn't really qualify him for a donation from *anybody*. After about an hour, he did manage to get another *"plonk"* in there, but in doing so he lost his *"plink"*. In the end, the security man from the store came out and moved him on, saying he was nothing but a plonker.

Luckily, Mum managed to persuade Inspector Lector to give them an advance on Ripley's wages, which solved their problems for the moment.

TWENTY-TWO

Jim

RIPLEY'S HANDLER AT the Dog Training School was a man called Jim, who looked about as old as Dad, and had thin hair and a nice smile, which is much better than a thin smile and nice hair (who'd want *fat* hair, anyway?). The family liked him right away.

Jim was actually the fifth choice of person to handle Ripley; others who were offered the job before him had all refused, on account of Ripley's reputation. Jim had only accepted it as long as the Police Department paid him fifty pounds a week extra as "danger money".

Jim was very kind but very strict, in equal measures, and in no time he gained Ripley's confidence; they became firm friends. There were no other Cockerpoos there, and Ripley was only there because he had a "special" talent. The first thing Jim taught him was how to knock on a door with the hard part of his tail. Then, he tried to get Ripley accustomed to loud noises. Now, we all know that Ripley was quite used to loud noises, due to his condition, but since a pistol shot was much louder than any noise *he* could make, they had to get him used to it. They did in the end, but it cost the Police Department about ten thousand pounds in ammunition. They put him through his weaving, jumping and scaling-high-walls routines, just in case he had to weave, jump or scale. Ripley would much rather have done "sit", "paw" and "scoff", but he had no choice – and he did get a treat every time he got it right.

The family began to notice changes in his behaviour, when he was home for the weekends. For example, he couldn't pass a chair without weaving through the legs, or approach a door without using his tail to knock on it. And, at every opportunity, he scaled – he took to scaling big time! He loved to scale his shed, to sit on the ridge of the roof. Sometimes he'd scale to the top of the kitchen cabinets, near to the ceiling. But each time he'd sit up there and bark to be rescued, because he hadn't yet learnt how to scale down again.

The family still hoped that Dad could find a job he liked,

so that Ripley could leave the police and wouldn't be put in any dangerous situation. But before Dad could, Ripley was called into action, when a woman called the police to say that some desperado was keeping an elderly couple hostage in their apartment.

Now, if *you've* ever held any elderly people hostage, you'll know that they can get quite annoyed with whoever "hostages" them. The elderly man had kicked the attacker in the unmentionables and disabled him, long enough to lift a window and shout to a passing woman that they were being held hostage:

"Sorry to bother you, but would you mind calling the police, please? Thank you very much."

The woman kindly obliged, and within no time four police cars and a vanload of officers in riot gear had blocked off the road outside.

Inspector Lector was in charge (not a Jammy Dodger in sight, but eyebrows working overtime), and shouting through a megaphone for the hostage-taker to come out.

"We have you surrounded. Come out with your hands up!"

But nobody did.

The hostage-taker could be seen through the windows, with what looked like a broom in his hand. To Inspector Lector it looked like a rifle.

"So he's armed, then?" he said.

"No, sir, it's a broom handle," replied a helpful constable.

"It's a rifle!" said Lector.

"If you look closer, sir, you can see the broom head."

"But it *might* be a rifle," said the inspector. "He needs to be disabled! Send for dog twenty-seven!"

Dog 27 was Ripley.

When Ripley arrived with his handler Jim, Lector briefed Jim on the situation and the "rifle", while all the constables behind Lector were shaking their heads, circling fingers at their temples, and miming sweeping with a brush whenever the word "rifle" was mentioned. Still, rifle or not, Jim had no choice but to enter the building with Ripley.

Once inside, Jim crouched behind a corner and watched, as Ripley went to the apartment door and knocked three times with his tail.

A woman came out and said: "Shoo!" So, Ripley went to the correct door this time and knocked again.

The door opened, Ripley stepped inside and the door closed again. It was just then that Jim realized he hadn't fed Ripley the meat he would need to aggravate his system and disable the guy.

Jim found himself with three choices:

*he could wait and see what happened...

*he could burst in and arrest the man...

or:

*he could eat the meat himself, and hope that it worked on him!

He decided to wait.

Ten minutes later, the door opened and Ripley came bounding out, followed by one of his best friends: Little John. It turned out that the elderly couple were Little John's great-grandparents, whom he was visiting and doing some cleaning for. His great-grandad was a little eccentric and forgetful; last time Little John had visited him, he opened the window and slid down a flagpole, thinking that he was a fireman.

The only good thing that happened that day was that Dad got a new job, in a Pickle Factory called "Perfect Pickles", where they pickled everything. They even pickled pickles. Dad was in charge of picking pickled peppers, to put precisely into the perfect pickling pods. The pay was good – twenty pounds a day and all the pickles he could eat – and with all the money that Ripley had earnt from the police force, it meant that Ripley could say goodbye to his police work.

Since he couldn't say goodbye himself, Mum did it for him. She thanked Inspector Lector and gave him a packet of Supreme Jammy Dodgers as a parting gift.

TWENTY-THREE
Visitors

NOW, TRY AS he might, Dad was frustrated that he hadn't come across much strangeness or mysteriousness lately. There was nothing strange or mysterious at the Pickle Factory, apart from the odd pickle or two which floated in the jar instead of sinking, and nothing strange happening anywhere else that he could see. Now he was suffering withdrawal symptoms, for a lack of things that were mysterious enough or strange enough to interest him.

He had already expounded all his theories about Ripley – i.e. that he was a throwback to prehistoric times, when pongs could kill, or that his mother might have escaped from an experimental laboratory, run by people who wanted to take over the world by dog-pong means – so he decided he needed to do a bit of "night research".

He decided this when he had been lying in bed for a couple of hours, and couldn't get to sleep. It had nothing to do with the fact that Mum was wearing a peg on her nose, to counteract the smell of pickles, and that the peg was making her snore; he was just in "mystery mode" and very restless.

So, he got up quietly, put on his dressing-gown with the *Star Trek* motifs, and tiptoed out into the back garden, where he stood looking at the stars for inspiration. All was quiet, except for a distant dog barking, which he thought might just be a call to all dogs in the vicinity to gather for an attack on something.

Then, he took the binoculars he always kept in his pyjamas pocket and began inspecting the sky, bit by bit.

Immediately, he gave an *"Ooooh!"* and became alert, as a huge, great, green globe came into view – but that turned out to be an apple, hanging on the tree they had by the shed.

Dad's *"Ooooh!"* had woken up Ripley, who staggered to the door, looked out, saw that it wasn't anybody about to feed him, so fed himself from his food contraption thing then went back to bed.

Dad spent another few disappointing minutes searching the sky, then decided he was wasting his time. Before he returned to the house, though, he did have another look at the apple, just in case it turned out to be a new planet that he'd discovered. It was definitely an apple.

He was about to enter the house, when the brightest of bright lights threw his own shadow onto the path in front of him. He froze. The hairs on the back of his neck stood on end and a cold shiver ran down his spine, reached his bottom, then turned round and ran back up again. Slowly, he turned. The bright light was streaming from an object descending slowly and silently beyond the back door, onto the adjacent field.

Dad's heart was racing. Stupefied with anticipation, he tottered to the back door and opened it. As he did so, the bright light went out, and he struggled to become accustomed to the darkness once again. When he finally focused, the sight which met him both frightened and excited him.

A circular metal object, about the size of a traffic island, stood in the field, its perimeter lights winking.

Dad shook his head in disbelief and his glasses fell off. He bent down to pick them up, and when he put them on again and looked, it was still there! Not only that, but a door was being lowered onto the grass, and two man-shaped creatures with swollen heads were stepping out! They sort of wobbled toward him and stopped about three metres away, looking at him with bug eyes, their long, thin arms, each with only three fingers, hanging well below their knobbly knees.

Dad's mind raced. What do you say to an alien? *Two* aliens, in fact. He was outnumbered!

He pointed over his shoulder with his thumb, and was about to squeak, "Fancy a cuppa?" when one of them spoke. And he spoke with a Birmingham accent!!

"Wiv cum fer thee dog."

"Eh?" said Dad, who had himself been born, bred and buttered in Birmingham.

"Smelly dog – tha' knows. Wiv cum fer it."

Dad gaped, but stood his ground.

"Yer can't 'ave it!" he said, in Birmingham-ese.

"Will see abaht that!" said the alien, and they both strode past him, over to Ripley's shed, and peered in before entering.

Dad watched, or rather listened, as the sounds of attempted abduction reached him where he stood, rooted to the ground, unable to move if he had wanted to. Had the aliens rendered him motionless, somehow? The noise in the shed grew steadily; Ripley seemed to be putting up a fight.

Suddenly, a very familiar sound (to Dad) ripped the air, as Ripley's rear end objected to what was happening. For a few seconds there was silence, then the aliens, one behind the other, fell through the door, got to their three-toed feet and staggered, on their spindly legs, back through the gate and into their spaceship. Within seconds, they were gone.

A voice crept its way into Dad's head:

"Robert! Robert! Wake up! You're going to be late for work!"

Dad breathed a sigh of relief and rolled out of bed.

TWENTY-FOUR
Pickle Pods

PART OF DAD'S new job was that, at the end of every month, he had to take the Pickle Factory's van and pick up a fresh load of pickle pods, as they arrived by boat at the port. He didn't mind doing that, as it got him out of the factory for a day, and it meant that when he got home he didn't smell quite so badly of pickles. Besides, there was a nice little "caff" down at the port, called Saucy Sue's, where he could get a cup of tea and a custard slice for £2.50 (25p cheaper than the local cake shop), and Dad *loved* custard slices.

On this particular pickle pod picking-up day, as he was leaving the house to collect the van from the factory, his eye caught Ripley, who was lying in his basket looking exceptionally fed-up. The kids were at school and Mum was at work. There was nobody about and it looked like he knew it. Dad felt sorry for him.

"Come on, Rippers," said Dad, and Ripley jumped to his feet, ready for anything.

All the way to the Pickle Factory in the car, and all the way to the port in the van, he had his daft head out of the window, his ears flying in the wind like a couple of kites, and his lips rattling on his teeth, like the sound of a floppy machine gun.

When they got there, the pickle pod boat had already arrived and Dad hurried over to it, leaving Ripley in the van, but completely forgetting to put the window up.

Ripley jumped out and went exploring (though it was less of an explore and more of a food-search). He toddled over to a fishing boat, which was just landing its catch on the quayside, and looked at what they had.

Crabs! Big crabs, with big pincer claws. Ripley quickly estimated their worth as a meal. He liked the smell of them, but not the way they were scuttling about – they were not, sort of, *dead* enough to eat.

As he was sniffing at them, one reached out and got a pincer-grip on his nose, as another attached itself to his ear. With a yelp, he jumped back and shook his head.

The one on his nose stayed gripped, but the one holding his ear flew off and landed on the bare back of a fisherman, who was bending to pick up a box. It was the man's turn to yelp as, quicker than you could say "nip", the crab slid down the back of his trousers.

Ripley didn't stay to see what followed. but instead took off, shaking his head from side to side until, eventually, the giant crab let go, fell to the floor, scuttled to the edge of the quay and splashed into the water. The crab fishermen didn't like that, and they told Ripley so with the brick they threw at him, which luckily he dodged.

Ripley's nose hurt, so he stuck it in a puddle to cool off. When he lifted it out again, he found it worked well enough to lead him to Saucy Sue's café, which smelled much more promising and looked a lot less dangerous.

He slipped inside as a customer opened the door to come out, looked around and made straight to a table occupied by four men – one very big and three smaller ones – who were shovelling food into their mouths, as though the world was going to end in less than five minutes.

The big one had a bushy white beard, bushy white

eyebrows and was wearing tiny, round spectacles. He could easily have been Santa on holiday and, as he looked down, Ripley put on his "please feed me" face, looking up.

"Hello, Doggy," said the man, cutting a morsel of meat and dropping it down to Ripley. Not five minutes later, one of "Santa's" elves dropped him another.

No need to tell you, dear reader, what happened next...

Dad, meanwhile, had loaded up his pickle pods and discovered that Ripley was no longer in the van. He panicked, because unless he got the packs of precious pickle pods back to the Pickle Factory, pronto, within a certain time they would go bad – then he'd be in a pickle and might lose his pickling job!

He searched around for Ripley, and more than one person thought it best to keep well away from him as, wild-eyed, he strode about shouting *"RIPPERS!"* at the top of his voice.

Not only was he anxious to prove that he could get the pickle pods back, pronto, but it was beginning to look like he might not get his custard slice at Saucy Sue's. The thought of the custard slice won out, and he made his way there, telling himself that Ripley might show up by the time he'd scoffed it.

What he didn't know was that, by now, Ripley was looking for *him*. He'd been chased from the café and was now wandering the port.

Needless to say, Dad didn't get his custard slice. What he did get was a shock, as he entered the café and saw all the bodies sprawled everywhere. Santa (if it was him) had his face in the remains of his dinner and (again, if it *was* him) didn't look as if he was going to be driving any reindeer for a couple of Christmases, at least. The place looked like the catering version of the Marie Celeste *(please look up "Marie Celeste" in order to fully understand this comparison – Author)*.

With barely a tear, Dad put his custard slice disappointment behind him and continued his search for Ripley.

Almost immediately, if not sooner, he found him…

The boat which had brought in the pickle pods was just leaving. The hoot that it gave as it pulled away drew Dad's attention, and there, standing in the stern of the boat, staring at him glumly, was Ripley!

Dad's mild panic (M.P.) jumped to Panic Full Blown (P.F.B.)! Eyes wild and white, sweating, he grabbed a passer-by, and nearly frightened the life out of him in doing so.

"That boat... there... there... that one..."

The man lost control of his bladder.

"WHERE'S ITS NEXT STOP?" Dad screamed.

The man slid to his knees in fright, but as he did so he managed to squeal: "Torquay!" This was followed by: "Don't kill me – I've got children!"

TWENTY-FIVE

Voyager

"TURKEY?!" CRIED MUM in disbelief. "Ripley's on a boat to Turkey?!!"

"So the man said," shrugged Dad.

"But that's..." began Erin.

"Nearly fifteen hundred miles away – I just checked!" said Jacob.

"What?! We'll never see him again!"

"Yes, we will!" cried Mum, with a confidence she didn't feel. But it was said with such spirited gusto, that nobody there would have been surprised if she had ripped off her pinny and revealed her Superwoman clothes underneath.

And so "Operation Gerrimback" was born; five determined pet owners on a desperate and dangerous mission, to retrieve their pet at all costs. Every spare minute – and even minutes that weren't spare – was put into the effort to get back their beloved, farty-bottomed dog.

Dad couldn't remember the name of the boat, but swore that one of the men on it looked, to him, like a dog-snatcher if ever he saw one. In another five minutes, if Mum hadn't shouted, "Oh, shush, Robert!" in a very loud voice, he would have had Ripley already sold in a Turkish market, in exchange for six camels.

They traced the shipping company which owned the boat, but the company insisted that they did not trade with Turkey, and if they decided to do so, they wouldn't be trading in pickle pods! Milly then had the idea that one of them should fly out to Turkey, and physically look for Ripley in all the ports there. But while Mum was looking up the cost of a flight to Turkey, Jacob discovered that Turkey had over a thousand ports – and that wasn't counting any of the Turkish islands.

It began to look as though they had run up against a brick wall. Well, all except Dad who, by this time, had convinced himself that the Russians had organized the whole thing and wanted Ripley for purposes of nerve-gas production.

*

AT THIS TIME, on the boat to Torquay, Ripley was feeling a little sorry for himself. He had tucked himself into a corner behind the wheelhouse, and the sway of the boat was giving him motion-sickness; this, in turn, was agitating his system. Luckily for the two-man crew, he hadn't had a great deal to eat – just the morsel that Santa (if it was him) had given him in the café. But even so, his efforts had made the wheelhouse windows fog over, and the pet parrot the boat's skipper always kept on a perch by the steering wheel had turned upside down and was now hanging by its claws, weakly imitating, and repeating over and over, the noise which had accompanied the pong that laid him out:

"Rrrrpp! Rrrrpp!"

The forward motion of the boat was sweeping most of Ripley's emissions toward the stern, and the crew were baffled as to why the wheelhouse windows had steamed up. And also, why today there were no seagulls anywhere to be seen. Did the birds know something that they didn't?

In a stroke of pure luck, the boat hit a stretch of calm water which helped calm Ripley's intestines, *just* as he was discovered in his corner by one of the crew – a young lad called Roland. Roland treated him kindly, gave him some water and read the address on his collar, realizing that he had strayed.

For the rest of the rip to Torquay, Ripley had the run of the boat and enjoyed standing in the prow, with the wind blowing in his face – a bit like that woman on the Titanic, in the film. At one point a blue dolphin swam alongside, and Ripley barked whenever its head popped up.

Suddenly, the dolphin jumped clean out of the water, twisted and splashed back in. Ripley was so thrilled that he gave a fart of joy. Now, dolphins are very intelligent creatures, and this might account for the fact that its next jump was made about half a mile away, after which it sped off.

Another hour's sailing brought them to Torquay harbour, where Roland decided he had to do something about getting Ripley back to his family. But, what?

*

BACK AT NUMBER 1 Gladioli Street, the family were in despair, and had spent a restless night wondering what they could do to get Ripley back from where they were sure he was headed: Turkey. That very morning, they had decided that they would all make the trip to London and approach the Turkish Embassy there for help. They had phoned the Embassy and got an official appointment with His Excellency the Turkish Ambassador, for two o'clock that afternoon.

They were all dressed for the occasion, to make a good impression: Dad with yet another new cap and *really* shiny shoes, Mum in the best dress she had, and the kids in stuff they hadn't had on since Aunt Polly's funeral, a year ago. The train fares had cost a fortune.

As they left the house, a white van drew up with a screech of brakes, as though the driver was in a great hurry. It was a courier delivery van. The driver shot out of his cab, wrenched open the back doors and reeled back in disgust. He then put on a hospital mask, reached into the van and pulled out a box with ventilation holes in it, and a red label on top which read: *"LIVE ANIMAL"*.

"Wigglesworth-Winterbottom?" he called, and offered Dad a page to sign. Dad did so.

"Yer might want t'pull yer Jerseys over yer nose!" he shouted, as he jumped back in the cab and drove off.

The sign on the van's rear doors caught Mum's eye:

*"FAST COURIER DELIVERY, **TORQUAY**."*

She looked at her husband. "Robert!!!" she said.

TWENTY-SIX
Missing

IT TOOK LONGER than before – about three months – for Ripley's system to settle down again, and another three months for them to be quite sure that his diet was working properly, but he was thriving now.

The no-meat diet had proved itself and he was "as happy as Larry", as the saying goes – though who Larry was, and why he was happy, I don't know, and I don't know anybody who does (if you know, please tell me).

Six months is a long time to expect anyone to remember what happened six months ago and, without reminders of why Ripley was famous, the memory of him began to fade in the public mind, if not in the public nose (though it hasn't been scientifically proven that noses have memories). The Fan Club gradually wound down until there was only Little John, very few regular members and no new ones at all. Still, the kids had made enough money by this time to buy

Mum a new washing machine and Dad a not-as-old car, *and* they had made enough to buy Joosyfroots to last a whole year, as long as they sucked instead of chewing them.

What happened next happened like this:

One Sunday morning, as usual, Jacob went out to the shed to fill Ripley's food contraption thing, and Ripley was nowhere to be seen. He wasn't in the shed, but then neither was he in the garden. He wasn't behind the wheelie bins (he sometimes lay there because he could smell food in them). He wasn't behind his favourite bush (which had droopy leaves, because he peed on it). He wasn't anywhere. What *was* there was a part-used roll of sticky duct tape, a torn bin bag, and a short length of rope with a frayed end.

Jacob reported back to the family.

"Maybe he jumped the fence?" suggested Milly.

"Why? He wouldn't! He doesn't do that anymore!"

"Well, he's gone and we'd better look for him!!" said Mum.

Dad took Jacob in the car to search the streets, while Erin and Milly combed all the parks, fields and butcher's shops for a mile around.

Half a day later, Ripley-less and exhausted, they met back at the house.

Dad checked the shed in case he'd come back. That was when he discovered the tape, bag and rope.

"What's this?" he asked Jacob.

"They were in the garden," replied Jacob, innocently.

"Why didn't you mention it?" growled Dad.

Jacob shrugged. "I didn't think it was important."

"Important?!" cried Dad. "Important?! This explains everything!" Dad had his *am-I-the-only-sane-person-around-here* look on his face, and a glint of "strange happenings" in his eyes.

"He's been kidnapped!!"

They all shuffled uncomfortably. This was obviously one of Dad's "mysterious happenings" fantasies.

"Robert..." warned Mum.

Dad brandished each item:

"This – the duct tape – to stop him barking; the bag they tried to put him in, but he tore it; the rope they tied him with, chewed through."

Doubt crept across their faces (but left no footprints).

Milly grabbed the sticky tape.

"Look," she cried, "that's his hair on the end!" And it was! Realization dawned.

"We have to tell the police – quickly!!"

*

THE SERGEANT AT the desk in the police station wasn't very sympathetic. He blinked rapidly when they said they'd come to report a stolen dog (rapid blinking is often a sign of complete disinterest, and the sergeant was doing a fair amount of blinking right now – very rapidly).

"Er... we don't, as a rule, investigate lost dogs, I'm afraid," he said, in a broad Welsh accent through a mouthful of bad teeth, whilst twiddling his pen and drumming his fingers.

"Stolen!" shot Erin. "Not lost!"

"Kidnapped!" said Jacob.

"Dognapped," put in Milly, precise as ever; "y'can't kidnap a dog. He's our dog and he's been napped!"

"Even, so young lady," said the sergeant, still twiddling

and drumming, "we can't waste police time looking for a kidnapped—"

"Dognapped!" shouted the three of them.

"—dog," continued the sergeant.

"But Ripley is a *special* dog, and after all he's done for you—" began Milly.

"Ripley?" said the sergeant. "You mean Ripley the Robber Stopper?"

"Yes!" they said in unison.

"My little girl's in his Fan Club!" said the sergeant. "This changes everything! Full details, please. We'll do what we can."

They gave a full description to the sergeant, who promised to circulate it to all patrol cars.

But the family left despondent – the world was full of black, curly dogs...

TWENTY-SEVEN
Diversions

WELL, IF I was to say that the next couple of weeks were unbearably miserable, I would *not* be fibbing, or even telling porkies.

*The kids couldn't concentrate on their schoolwork…

*Mum kept giving out wrong dinner combinations, like custard with chips, or she'd ask pupils would they like sugar on their sausage, or vinegar on their apple pie… and:

*When they got home each day there was no happy, bouncy dog to meet them…

It was as though all meaning had gone out of life. After a good while, it became clear to the children that they had two choices – either:

1) Be despondent and grieve until they died, over what had happened…

or:

2) Try to distract themselves in some way, in an effort to ease the pain of not having Ripley around anymore...

Mum and Dad felt the same sadness but, being adults, they could handle it better.

Jacob decided that he'd try to distract himself with ice skating, which he'd had some experience of a few years ago. He arranged with his mates to go to the rink in the next town, but when he got there he discovered that, in his distracted state, he'd packed his rollerblades by mistake, and had to spend a whole two hours watching his friends having fun. He tried to hire a pair from the rink, but they had none in his size, which wasn't surprising since Jacob had a pair of the biggest feet you have ever seen – size 16+! – with toes like mini bananas; so big that when he went swimming he had no need to wear flippers. He took an early bus home and, when he got there, he found himself even more depressed than he had been when he left!

Sporty Erin was a player for both her local under-14s football team *and* the under-14s rugby team in the town; it was football on a Saturday and rugby on a Sunday most weeks. This particular Saturday, she trotted onto the pitch with only half her mind on what she was doing. Normally, she could be counted upon to score at least one goal and to assist in the scoring of others, but this Saturday was different. Not only did she play the rottenest game of her life, but she managed to score *seven* own goals! Then, at one point, when the ball came over from a corner, she caught it and went sprinting up the field. She got as far as the halfway line before she realized it was Saturday, not Sunday!

Milly didn't fare any better. She loved her dancing, and was more than competent in all the dance routines she had learnt, including being ballet-trained. But at one ballet lesson she was told off three times by the teacher for not having her mind on her work. She pulled herself together, but then, during a session at the bar, when all the class where in a line and on one leg, she performed a "fouetté" instead of an "arabesque", and knocked everyone down like a row of skittles.

Regular checks with the police station were fruitless, and regular searches of the area and beyond came to nothing.

Then, one evening, a news item came on the telly about a jewel robbery somewhere, in which the thieves had used… a dog!

What??!!

That was it – no further details.

But the newspapers the next day had the full story…

According to *The Daily Posh*:

"…thieves had shoved a dog into a jeweller's shop, carrying a device (probably attached to its collar) which released a knockout gas. Once the gas had disabled the staff, the thieves had donned gas masks, entered the premises and taken all the jewels."

The Daily Fib got it right. In big letters on the front page:

"FART-DOG ROBS JEWELLERS!!

Famous robber-catcher dog Ripley, who hit the headlines for apprehending thieves by breaking wind, has turned his talents to the other side of the law..."

It was bad news, but it was still news, and the family's spirits rose. He was alive!

Interest in the doings of Ripley was quickly revived, and dozens of Fan Club members (and those who now wanted to be Fan Club members) immediately got in touch. Most of them, unbelievably, wanted to know why Ripley, who had previously *caught* burglars, was now *helping* them – as though Ripley had decided himself to do so! Some people, eh?

Anyway, the police sat up and took notice, and began a search for Ripley and his robber mates. They also came to the house, all unnecessarily flashy-blue and *"nee-naw"*, led by Inspector Lector, who saw the chance of another fix of Jammy Dodgers. He managed six, and stuffed another three in his pocket while quizzing the family, but soon gave up when he realized that the family had no more idea where Ripley was than he had himself.

Now, anybody with a brain larger than a pea might be

forgiven for thinking that things couldn't get much worse. Why? Because:

*your beloved pet dog is in the hands of criminals…

and:

*he is being used to commit crime!!

and:

*your dad is coming home each day smelling of pickles…

How much worse do you want?!

But actually, things were about to get *much* worse! About a-hundred-and-fifty times much worse! Or more!

And, if you don't believe that could be, read on!

TWENTY-EIGHT
Four "NO"s

AUDITIONS FOR THE famous *X Factor* show were taking place in the next town (no, *that's* not the "much worse" I was talking about), and the auditions were taking place in front of a live audience (a *dead* audience wouldn't have known what was happening), but there was no transmission involved – i.e. there were no cameras.

With the news of Ripley's involvement in the jewel raid fast fading, and still no news of him being found, glumness had settled in the house like a big, black glum vulture settles on a carcass, so Mum suggested the kids might go along to the auditions, to occupy their minds in a less glummy way.

They took Little John with them. He was missing Ripley as much as they were. Utterly miserable, they sat in the balcony and watched.

The first act was a juggler, and he juggled (of all things) flour! Not bags of flour, as you might expect, but handfuls of loose, powdery flour. He tried to sing a flour-themed song at the same time – something about *"Flowers in the Spring"*, but only ended up coughing and spluttering. When he'd done, the stage looked like Santa's Grotto, and it took the stage crew half an hour to clean up! The judges weren't impressed and they gave him four *"NO"*s.

Next was a man playing keepy-uppy with a football... then two footballs... then... three? He was doing quite well until one of the balls flew off and hit Dec, standing in the wings. It was travelling at some speed when it bounced off Dec's head and whacked Amanda, one of the lady judges, full in the face, splattering her perfect lipstick all over her perfect nose, relocating an eyelash to her perfect cheek and knocking her perfect wig off. She was not pleased. The footballer got *five "NO"*s, including one from Amanda and another from her wig.

Act three was a very good singer, who sang about 25 verses of a slow church hymn, and would have sung 26 verses, if he had been able to hear himself above the snores of the audience. He got no score because the judges were asleep.

Things got a bit interesting when act four came on. It was a dog act. Judge Simon woke up and was all smiles – he loved dog acts. Two burly, unshaven men came on carrying a bag and leading a black, curly dog…

Milly, Jacob, Erin and Little John sat up, sharply.

"There's Ripley!" said Little John loudly, and people around shushed him.

"Ripley," whispered Little John.

From this distance, the dog did look very like Ripley. But it couldn't be – what would he be doing here? Yet…

"What are your names?" asked Simon.

"Errm… I'm Fingers and he's Mugsy," grunted one of them.

Simon looked puzzled. "And your doggy friend?"

The pair grinned at each other through broken teeth. "Moneybox. We call him Moneybox."

"Any reason for that?" asked Simon.

They chuckled. "Yeah," they answered, but didn't say why.

"Okay," said Simon, "show us what you can do."

With that, the two dipped into their bags, brought out a

gas-mask each, put them on and just stood there, looking at their watches. The dog licked his chops and lay down, miserably, between them. Then… nothing happened.

The kids were the only people in the whole theatre who had made the connection between the masks, the dog and the unsavoury characters now on stage.

"They've fed him meat!! Stop them!" shouted Milly.

"That's our dog!" cried Erin.

But their voices were lost, in the torrent of objections from the people around them.

The judges were looking at each other, puzzled. The puzzled audience looked at each other, puzzled, and began to get more puzzled. And the ruckus from the balcony was puzzling people even more.

Another couple of puzzling minutes passed, then there was a sudden thud as Ant fell out of the wings, flat on his face, to be followed by another thud as he was followed by Dec (those two always do things together). On seeing this, there was an *"Oohhh!"* from the audience. This was followed moments later by a flurry of *"Oh, my goodness!"* as, one by one, the four judges collapsed onto their desk.

Amanda lost her wig again and Simon went, *"Oooh!"* as his pen went right up his nose.

The two men on stage exchanged a wink and a nod.

Although the pong hadn't reached the balcony, the kids watched in horror as it spread through the downstairs audience, row by row. People slumped in their seats, slid to the floor or toppled forward.

After about ten rows it seemed to lose power, because rows eleven and twelve just reeled dizzily, but didn't collapse.

Then the two men on stage went into action.

Not only that, but from the exit doors came four others, also masked up. The six of them went along the rows of flaked-out people, taking watches, rings, necklaces and anything else they could find which looked valuable. They even took one man's hearing aid.

At this point, the kids, the balcony audience, and those of the downstairs audience who could still move, decided to leg it. Trouble was, everybody tried to get through the same door at the same time and Erin, the smallest, could have got seriously injured if Little John hadn't put her over his shoulder and carried her out (Erin nearly died of shame, because her knickers were showing).

Once outside, the *"nee-naw"* of approaching police sirens could be heard in the distance, as people streamed off in all directions.

"Quick!" cried Milly. "Stage door, round the corner!"

She was right: it was the only way out for the thieves.

And sure enough, there they were, piling into a black van with their loot – and, of course, Ripley.

"RIPLEEEY!" they all shouted.

Ripley took one look, gave a joyful bark, and immediately strained toward them on his rope, a look of hope and joy on his bushy face. One cruel yank on the rope brought him back, then he was picked up and thrown in the van. Doors slammed and it began to move off.

Little John, weeping with anger, ran after it. He then stopped, picked up a stone and threw it, as hard as he could. It smacked against the back windscreen and cracked it.

As the van screeched around the corner, they saw Ripley's sad little face peering out at them... then he was gone.

TWENTY-NINE
Hope

WHEN THEY GOT home, Mum and Dad knew all about what had happened from the radio. Little John was still furious, and had already made his mind up that he was going to search everywhere, until he found the van with the cracked windscreen. They couldn't persuade him otherwise and he had gone off, very angry and very determined.

"You didn't get the registration number?" asked Dad.

"Something with a 'Y' in it, I think," offered Milly, dejectedly.

"And it was black," said Erin. Then she added: "Poor Ripley."

There was silence for a while (except for Erin sobbing), then Jacob piped up: "I've got an idea."

The news didn't fill the others with joy.

"Didn't you hear what I said?" exclaimed Jacob.

"An idea," muttered Milly, then, "what idea?!"

"We need to find a black van, right, with a cracked back windscreen and possibly a Y in its registration?"

They looked at him blankly. "And?"

"The Fan Club! Let's message the Fan Club and ask them to search for it!"

"Jacob," said Dad, "sometimes, you're not as daft as you look!"

"Thanks," said Jacob, mistaking it for a compliment.

Erin and Milly were already at the computer, and in less than ten minutes the message was on its way:

"CALLING ALL RFC MEMBERS!
HELP!
RIPLEY IN DANGER! RIPLEY IN DANGER!
BE ON THE LOOKOUT FOR A BLACK VAN,
CRACK IN REAR WINDSCREEN, POSSIBLE 'Y'
IN THE REG.
CONTACT IMMEDIATELY!!!!"

And so, hope once again shone in their eyes.

The very same hope began to fade from their eyes when,

by bedtime, there had been no reports of black van sightings.

Someone had, however, seen:

*a *blue* van with a Y in the reg…

Someone else had spotted:

*a *red* van with a cracked rear windscreen…

A fan in China had seen:

*a rickshaw which was black…

and another had seen:

*a *very dark grey* van, with a Y in the reg *and* a cracked windscreen – but it was the *front* windscreen which had the crack.

Hope died completely after three days of nobody seeing anything, and they actually *buried* hope three weeks later.

R.I.P. HOPE.

No, that doesn't say *"rip"* hope; it means *"rest in peace"* hope, just so you're sure.

There was little they could do except keep their own eyeballs peeled (it doesn't hurt) and go searching every street they had ever walked down, even walking down streets they didn't have to and back up again. But no black van.

The police said they were expecting another raid by the thieves – though, of course, they didn't know where. But "Operation Ripley" was put on alert and was waiting, engines revving. Inspector Lector had polished his whistle until he could see his face in it *(ugh!)*, and had filled the pockets in his stab vest with emergency Jammy Dodgers, just in case.

But when the breakthrough finally came, it was not from the direction of the police. Hope was dug up again (still in good condition) about a month after the *X Factor* raid, when a knock on the door revealed a very dishevelled Little John who, once he got his breath back, shouted very loudly, through a huge grin: "I've found the van!!"

Apparently, he had hardly been home for a whole month, except for dinners and bed, and had spent every minute of every day searching backstreets and garages – all for the love of Ripley. What a hero!

THIRTY
The Search

LITTLE JOHN WAS desperate to show them where the van was *right now*, and anxious, in his innocence, to be reunited with his beloved Ripley, but they could see that he was exhausted from his search. They managed to sit him down and gave him a slice of his fave cake (lemon sponge) and a cup of hot tea, then made him go straight home, sucking on a tube of Frootyshoots, for a shower and some sleep, saying they'd call on him.

"Bless him!' said Mum. "Now we're getting somewhere! We'll call the police."

"And tell 'em what?!" asked Dad.

"Well..." She slapped her forehead (though it wasn't her forehead's fault). "We didn't ask Little John where the van was!"

They decided to wait a couple of hours before calling on him for the address – it was the least they could do, considering what he'd done for them.

When Milly and the twins got round to his house, it was no surprise to find that he had been waiting for them for over an hour. His mother had to lock the door to keep him in, and met them with the disturbing news that John had forgotten the name of the street where the van was.

"Can you show us?" asked Milly.

John nodded vigorously, and ten minutes later all four of them strode out, just as night fell *(clang!)* on the town.

Little John took them down a maze of backstreets; streets they didn't know existed in the town, and some streets they would never have gone down even if they *had* known they existed. Little John stomped confidently through the alleys, each one imprinted on his mind from his search, then stopped abruptly and pointed. There, right in front of them, in the scruffy back courtyard of an old, ramshackle house, they saw it: the very van! Black, with a crack in the rear windscreen.

"No Y in the reg.," muttered Jacob.

"Sorr-eee!" mumbled Milly scornfully, then fished her phone out and began punching numbers.

"There's a light in that window," whispered Erin. "Let's look."

"I'm calling the police," said Milly.

"Look, we're here now," said Erin. "They could scarper before the police get here!"

"Then I'm calling Mum and Dad," continued Milly. "They think we only went to Little John's to talk to him."

But already Erin was creeping toward the window, and Jacob and Little John were following. With a sigh, Milly shoved the mobile in her pocket and went after them. The curtain across the window had not been closed properly and, through the gap, they made out four men sitting around a table littered with beer cans. Ripley was nowhere to be seen.

The men were obviously planning something. The one called Fingers was stabbing his finger at what looked like a map, and tracing the same finger away to somewhere else – the thought crossed Milly's mind that maybe that was why he was called Fingers.

It wasn't possible to hear clearly what was being said, but Milly mouthed the word "bank" to the others.

"Yeah?" whispered Jacob. "Like the Y in the reg.?"

"Shurrup!" she said. "And listen."

They listened... and listened... The odd words got through to them, like "nuff said" and "gizza fag", but what they *did* hear, clearly, was a loud, gruff and intimidating voice behind them, saying, "What we got 'ere, then?" followed by a nasty-man growl.

They spun and gasped in unison, as the man called Mugsy – big and ugly and beefy, with a wart on his nose – advanced, blocking the way out. With about as much gentleness as a wild bear might show to something edible, he herded them to the door, kicked it open and shoved them inside.

"Look what I got!" he grunted. "They've been listening at the window."

Next thing they knew, they were pounced on (Little John needed pouncing on by *two* of them, and even then they needed a big pounce) and bundled away, to a small room which smelled of damp and was full of cobwebs and boxes.

Cramped, tied and gagged with old rags that tasted of

oil, the four kids were dumped against the wall, the door was slammed and they were left to their own thoughts in the dark, unable even to talk to each other. No amount of struggling and pulling could loosen their hands, and things soon began to look hopeless.

*

DAD AND MUM had waited until ten p.m., even though it went dark at about nine, before slipping from anxiety to a full-blown parent-panic. This was quite an achievement, considering that some parents have been known to panic if their child is thirty seconds late coming home from school.

At eight o'clock they had gone to Little John's house and found his mum in a similar state of worry, but with knobs on! From there they called the police, even though Little John's mum had called them twice already – once at five and again at six. The phone was still steaming on her lap when they got there.

What was particularly worrying was that none of the kids had used their mobiles. Dad, for once, had not attached any mysteriousness to all this – no mention of aliens or unexpected happenings, no conspiracy theories or suspicions; this was a serious matter. His children were missing.

Right now, the three of them – Mum, Dad and Little John's mum, Agnes – were sitting, zombified, in number 1 Gladioli Street, on their fourteenth cup of tea, with a plateful of uneaten but very comforting chocolate digestives on the table.

"They'll be back any minute," said Dad.

The two mums nodded and stared at the wallpaper which, Agnes had discovered, had no less than thirty-two flowers on the wall with the fireplace – she'd counted them twice.

There was a knock at the door (even though they did have a doorbell) and Dad banged his knee on the coffee table *("OW!")* in his rush to answer it.

There were two policewomen on the doorstep, one large and one small. Large Policewoman narrowed her eyes, though they were quite narrow to start with – in fact, if anyone had ever wanted to blindfold her, for some reason, they could have done it with a shoestring.

"Matter of missing children, sir?"

THIRTY-ONE
Rats and Stuff

IN THE ROBBERS' hideout, throughout that night, no one slept.

As the hours went by, in dark, damp silence, scratching noises in a corner of the room began to make them think that they were not the room's only occupants. Once, something furry ran across Milly's hands, causing her to give a muffled scream, like: *"Eurrrrgh!"* As muffled screams go, it was not a bad attempt. Their biggest worry was not being able to tell their parents what had happened; even if they had managed to free their hands, the robbers had taken their mobiles off of them.

They knew that their parents would have alerted the police by now, but what good was that when nobody knew where they were? *They* didn't even know where they were!

It was early the next morning, light filtering through cracks and gaps, that they heard movement in the house and muffled voices, and dreaded what might come next. But no one came in to them, and maybe an hour later they heard the van start up and move away.

Shortly after this, knowing *something* must be done, with a superhuman effort, a good set of teeth and use of the corner of a box, Milly managed to free the gag around her mouth. Then, using the same teeth (they were the only ones she had), she also managed to untie the knot on Jacob's hands. Twenty minutes later (Jacob was rubbish at knots) everybody was free.

Free, but trapped in the room. The door was locked, but then they didn't expect anything else. It had four panels thinner than the rest of the door, and Little John, with his height and strength (and feet even bigger than Jacob's), managed to kick a panel out. But the door remained locked, and had no key in the lock on the other side, that they might have been able to reach. However, with the panel missing, they were all able to get handholds on the edge of the gap and jerk the door backward and forward, until the lock broke.

They tumbled into the main room and raced for the front

door, but *that* was locked – and this was a heavy, solid door. Tears came to Erin's eyes. "We'll never get out of here!"

"Yes, we will," grunted Little John; "watch me." And he heaved at the door handle. The handle came off in his hand and they all stared, numbly, at each other.

"We... we just have to think it through," said Milly, trying to sound as hopeful as she could, as she sat wearily at the table (unbelievable as it may sound, dear reader, none of them had ever broken out of a house before, after being tied up and gagged overnight).

On the table was the map that the thieves had been planning their job with. Milly took one look and called the others over. She pointed at the map, on which a circle had been drawn around a bank.

"That's the bank in the High Street," said Jacob.

"Exactly! That's their target!"

"I've got my money in there, that I got from Aunty Polly for Christmas!" said Erin, angrily.

"How much?" asked Little John.

"Three-pounds-fifty."

"Wow!" said Little John, seriously impressed.

"What time is it?" asked Milly.

Jacob looked. "Two o'clock. Why?"

Milly's eyes were gleaming now. "What would be the best time to rob a bank, d'y'think?"

"Dunno... when it's closed?"

"No, dummy! Too difficult to get in!"

"Oh, I see... best when it's open, then...? Let's see... dunno."

"When there's hardly anyone there!" she said. "When the bank is *about* to close."

Jacob shrugged. "Suppose... yeah."

"And the banks close at three o'clock," continued Milly. She gave them all one of her meaningful looks (she had plenty left). "We've got one hour!"

Just then, there was the smashing of glass, as Little John threw a chair through the window.

THIRTY-TWO

Snared

FIFTEEN MINUTES OF fast running got them home.

They found Mum, Dad and Little John's mum worried out of their minds, half-finished teacups all over the table, and bitten fingernails all over the floor. There were gasps of relief when they tumbled in like a pack of frightened goats, jabbering and gesticulating, ignoring all of the *"Where've you been?"*s and *"You had us so worried!"*s, in their desperation to tell their story.

Hugs and smothering kisses were pushed away, and they all began shouting at once – all except Little John, who was so pleased to see his mum that he picked her up and swung her around, before tripping over a rug and depositing her in the fireplace. After that, the kind person that he was, he swept up the fingernails that their parents had all been chewing, and collected the teacups for washing.

The two policewomen had come back, too, reporting

that, after a night's search, they had not been found. Now Large Policewoman rose to her feet, anxious to get things in perspective, notebook in hand.

"So, these *are* the missing children?"

"We were – not now," said Erin.

Before anything else could be said, Milly cried: "The High Street bank is about to be robbed!"

Immediately, silence descended. (Silence tends to descend very quickly and very quietly, as a rule, and this silence was no exception.)

"How do you know that?" Large Policewoman asked, in a voice so suspicious that Dad almost asked for her autograph.

Then the whole story came out, as quickly as they could tell it: finding the van; their capture; their escape; and the discovery of the plan that the robbers had made. It was when they showed the rope marks on their wrists that they began to be believed, and Large Policewoman turned to Small Policewoman and agreed, with serious nods, that they should pass on the information.

(It's worth noting that no policeperson will ever take

any action without giving a least two serious nods. I tell you this just so that you'll know the minute you're about to be booked for something you might not have realized you'd done - Author.)

So it was that Operation Ripley got the green light and, in a mad scramble worthy of the start of a Grand Prix, every patrol car at the station roared into action – except one, which had been ready and revving for so long that it had run out of petrol. Large and Small Policewomen allowed the kids to travel in their patrol car.

I have to tell you here that none of the patrol cars actually *looked* like patrol cars; no markings or "flashy blues" on them, because this would have scared the robbers off. The patrol cars consisted of:

*a 1960s Ford Anglia, with a missing back bumper…

*a fish van (belonging to the father of one of the policemen, and which smelled very badly)…

*two tractors off the farm by the police station…

*a Citroen C.V. with two-tone paintwork: green and rust…

and:

*a three-wheeled Robin Reliant (with a trailer)…

There was supposed to have been a hearse as well (minus coffin), belonging to an ex-policeman who was now a funeral director, but it got a puncture on the way.

And all the policemen inside them wore plain clothes – well, almost all: Inspector Lector wore a bit of a snazzy jumper with *"JUST DO IT"* on the front, and his police cap turned back to front.

Altogether, nine disguised patrol cars, full of disguised policemen, trundled in a line to the town square, and parked either opposite the bank or around the block from where the bank stood, waiting. And then waiting some more… Flasks of tea, cheese sandwiches... then more waiting.

It was five minutes to closing time when the black van cruised into the street and found a convenient parking space – conveniently just where the police had left them one.

THIRTY-THREE
Retribution

THE VAN DOOR slid open and Mugsy's fat stomach popped out, followed by Mugsy himself, then Fingers, then two more heavy, scrub-headed, tattooed men, one of them leading Ripley on a piece of rope. They tried hard to look casual – just four bloaty-bellied, ordinary, criminal-looking men walking their doggy – but the more casual they tried to look, the more suspicious they looked, and they had already looked *very* suspicious before all this.

"Prepare to move," crackled Inspector Lector's voice, over the intercom in the kids' car.

"Wait!" cried Milly.

"We have it covered, Miss!" warned the officer in front of her.

"But... please... they will have given Ripley his meat by now! If he goes off, no one will be safe!'

The officer chewed his lip; he'd had no breakfast, and

would've chewed anything at that moment.

"Good point, Miss," he said. Then, into the microphone: "Suspects must be detained *before* they enter the building! Skip along! Skip along! Skip along!"

"Skip along?!" asked Jacob. "Don't you mean, 'Go! Go! Go!'?"

"We like to keep it polite, son," said the officer.

Four officers from each car (except one who had fallen asleep waiting, and another who still hadn't finished his last cheese sandwich) sprang into action and raced for the robbers. Suddenly, the odds against the robbers became... erm... let's see... four men... nine cars... that's thirty-six... and... The odds against the robbers became 9 to 1 (minus the officer still asleep). The odds jumped to 10 to 1, when the officer who still had a sandwich to finish finished it and joined his mates. At the same time, the four kids jumped out, making it... erm... 12 to 1... probably...

At the very door of the bank, in the very act of putting on their gas masks, the robbers saw the horde of disguised policemen racing toward them, headed by a mad-eyed bloke with a moustache, waving a stick and shouting,

"CHAAAARGE!" with what looked like bits of biscuit flying out of his mouth. The robbers gulped, dropped their masks and scrambled, with Ripley, through the glass door, into the lobby of the bank.

Inside, there was another door into the bank itself, which they tried, unsuccessfully, to open. This was because, cleverly, the bank staff had been told by the police to lock it – good, eh? So, there they were, trapped in the small space that was the foyer of the bank – with Ripley, who was primed to *deliver*. Everyone gathered and watched, as realization melted the faces of the robbers.

Fingers tried to use his fingers to edge the door open and push Ripley out, but Large Policewoman With Narrow Eyes put her weight against the door, nipping Fingers's fingers, sealing their fate and putting a smile on Large Policewoman's face, which made her eyes actually disappear.

Ripley had no choice but to do what they had intended him to do and, when he did... well, some of the policepersons had to turn away to hide their very merriment. *(Policepersons are not supposed to show enjoyment at other people's misfortunes, but sometimes it's difficult not to.)*

The robbers jumped up and down!

They:

*shouted…

*ran about wildly…

*coughed…

*choked…

*gagged…

*vomited…

*screamed…

*pleaded…

*dribbled..

*slid contorted faces against the glass, leaving snot trails…

*banged on the doors, eyes rolling wildly and mouths sagging…

Then…

One by one they fell to their knees, sobbing, before passing out, clutching their throats.

When they did so, Ripley climbed onto the bum of face-down Fingers, looked at the kids through the glass and put his daft face on, tongue hanging.

It was four hours and six Jammy Dodgers later before Inspector Lector reckoned it was safe to open the door. Every hour they had to push a Smellometer under the door, to check the pong level, and even when it was declared safe they had to wear masks. All that time, Ripley pressed himself against the glass as Milly, Jacob, Erin and Little John did the same on the other side and talked to him. When they finally let him out, he licked them all until his tongue was dry, and continued to do so all the way home in the police car.

THIRTY-FOUR
Normality

ONCE AGAIN, RIPLEY'S name was on everybody's lips (though not his *full* name, Ripley Wigglesworth-Winterbottom, because everybody would've had to have *that* name right across their cheeks, as well. Yes, Ripley was once again a national hero, and the Queen announced that he would be given a Certificate of Doggy Merit. Not *the* Queen – not actually Her Very Majesty the Queen – but a drag artiste in a local bar called Queenie Renée, who had been following Ripley's story... but the thought was the same. They had the presentation in the pub, where Queenie made it the centrepiece of her act.

Back at home once more, it took a little while for Ripley's digestive system to get back to normal, and to accept a meatless diet once more, and there were one or two small emergencies whilst this happened. For example, there was another evacuation of the living room just two days after he came back, but on a much smaller scale than before. And then, about a week later, on a walk with Jacob, a big, unaccompanied, growling dog, with a spiky collar and teeth like fork prongs, approached them. It was snarling and dripping saliva, and Jacob feared for his life – not only his knees but his elbows were knocking. Slowly, it crept toward them on its huge paws, and there was no doubt that it was in attack mode. It stopped about two metres from them and shifted its weight onto its back quarters – a sure sign that it was about to spring. This dog, obviously, had never heard of Ripley, or it wouldn't have been there at all – all it saw was a juicy, black dog and an even juicier boy, both just waiting to have its fangs sunk into them.

To this day, Jacob swears that Ripley *purposely* (and for the last time ever, though neither of them knew that then) produced what was left of his special ability, as a defence mechanism. The dangerous dog froze in its tracks. Its eyes widened, its nose wrinkled, its ears shot up… then it yelped, and ran off so fast that sparks flew from its toenails.

From that day on, Ripley became a perfectly normal, pong-free pet. It was everything that the family had ever wanted, and it was as welcome as a breath of fresh air.

More and more people wanted to join his Fan Club. He appeared on the front cover of *Vegans Monthly* – and got paid for it! Milly, Jacob and Erin were, in fact, able to pay one of his most ardent fans – a girl from Barking, in Essex – to run his Fan Club, and she was helped by another girl from *Dog*enham. The kids were able to afford this because a wonderful thing happened…

An important-looking letter had arrived from the High Street bank's Head Office, asking if Mr. and Mrs. Wigglesworth-Winterbottom would be kind enough to visit the Executive Director at their convenience. Dad wasn't sure about this because, as far as he could remember, from his early days in Birmingham, "convenience" had always been an alternative word for "toilet" (as in: "Can I please use your convenience?"), and he couldn't help but wonder why they had to meet at the toilet.

Wearing their best clothes, they all travelled to London, first-class train fares paid, to meet the Executive Director – a tall, thin man called Mr. Gorralot, who had gold-rimmed glasses, a number of gold teeth, several gold rings and a

100-pound note sticking out of his top pocket, where other people might wear a handkerchief *(handkerchiefs were things that people blew their noses on before tissues were discovered – again, just so you know).*

(Just a random thought here, on discoveries: I wonder what electric eels were called before electricity was discovered? Answers on a ten-pound note, please, to the author.)

Anyway, Mr. Gorralot had some very good news: as a reward for the children saving their bank from being robbed, he revealed that they would be giving the family a whopping big sum of money, to be split into payments each year for the next ten years!

Whoopee, thought the kids, when they heard about it. *Joosyfroots forever!*

But the money bought more than Joosyfroots. It made it so that Dad could afford to work part-time, and this would substantially lessen the pickle-whiff, as well as leaving him more time to pursue his hobby: strangeness.

Mum could have given up work, too, but decided not to because, she said, she would miss the smell of school dinners. This was when Milly seriously thought that her mum had lost her mind.

Another pleasant happening happened to happen, when they happened to be contacted by a man who wanted to promote a new diet he had invented, and was desperate to get permission from them to call it "Ripley's A1 Dietary Mixture". This man, Mr. Ivor Wobblybottom, offered to pay them for the use of Ripley's name, and the family found it very hard to say no – so they didn't. The A1 Dietary Mixture went on to be very successful, and provided large ladies with yet another reason to eat dumplings and cream cakes without fear of putting on weight, because they were taking A1.

By this time, Dad had bought:

*an infra-red camera, to snap any strange happenings in the dark…

*a device to track shape-shifters (with an extra-fast shutter, to catch them just as they shifted)…

And:

*a transmitter which sent coded beeps into space, saying: *"Follow this signal for a toasted teacake."*

Mum had to buy a new wardrobe, and the kids had so many Joosyfroots that they couldn't close the door on their secret Joosyfroots cupboard, which also doubled as an old rabbit hutch.

Life was good – and about to get better, they thought...

THIRTY-FIVE

Titled

ONE MORNING, SOON after, Ripley padded into breakfast with the morning post in his mouth. He'd been doing this ever since the day the postman had left a free sample of shampoo, in a sachet which had smelled to him like chocolate. He had chewed it and liked it, but spent the next three days blowing soapy bubbles from both ends of his anatomy. It hadn't happened since, but Ripley kept hoping that it would, and had gotten into the habit of checking the post every day.

On this particular day, amongst the bills, all the junk mail and the free coupons, was an envelope which stood out for its sheer quality. It was made from cream-coloured cartridge paper (dead good, expensive stuff) and had an embossed crest in gold, in the top left-hand corner. Dad recognized it straight away as the crest of Her Very Majesty the Queen.

"It's from Buckingham Palace," he said, in awe.

It was addressed to:

"Ripley Wigglesworth -Winterbottom,

c/o Mr. and Mrs. Wigglesworth -Winterbottom,

1, Gladioli Street,

Harbington."

Mum's jaw dropped. "Her Very Majesty," she whispered, "writing to Ripley?!"

They opened the envelope carefully, aware that Her Very Majesty might have actually licked the sticky bit with her own very Royal tongue. The letter inside, once again on exquisite paper, was from Her Majesty's Private Secretary, telling them that:

"For services rendered, Her Majesty would like it to be known that Ripley Wigglesworth-Winterbottom is to be bestowed with the honour of Knight of the Garter..."

The family were stunned and Dad's deepest suspicions were aroused, especially about the word "garter". He became convinced that it was a typo, and that whoever had typed it had meant the G to be an F. He even looked at his keyboard and pointed out that F was right next to G – what more proof did anyone want?

But everything else about it seemed genuine, down to the Queen's signature at the bottom:

"Elizabeth II Regina."

There was a phone number for them to ring, to accept the invitation, and Mum, after a strong cup of tea to steady her nerves, put on her poshest voice and rang it.

An even posher voice answered:

"Her Majesty's Private Secretary."

"Good heevening," said Mum, timidly. "Hi ham in possession hov a letter from you habout ha hinvest... errrm... a hin..."

"Investiture?" asked the Private Secretary.

"Hexactly," stuttered Mum.

"And your name is...?"

"Hi ham Mrs. Wigglesworth-Winterbottom."

"Aahh," said the man, "the owner of Ripley."

He went on to confirm that the invitation was genuine, and gave her the date and time at which they must present themselves at the Palace.

"One other thing, Mrs. Wigglesworth-Winterbottom," the Personal Secretary went on to say: "please keep this a secret until the official announcement is made."

Well, it took two days for the news to sink in and for Dad to admit (reluctantly) that he had been wrong about the G being an F. It was almost as though they were afraid that, if they accepted that it was true, it would turn out to be a dream.

"*'Sir'* Ripley of Harbington? Really?!"

But, once they had gotten used to it, it was full speed ahead to be ready for the day: what to wear, how to get there, what they'd do *when* they got there, etc., etc... The keeping-it-secret bit didn't last long, when Erin let it slip to her schoolfriends 'cos she was so proud, and got ribbed in return...

"Yer what?" they'd say. "Getting knighted for farting?"

Erin argued fiercely that it was for all the charity work

he'd done, apart from his help in catching criminals, but the ribbing continued:

"So, he'll be Sir Ripley of Gladioli Street, will he? Will he have a posh bark?"

That was when Erin lashed out and gave the girl who said it a big, red hand-mark on her cheek – and got detention for it.

It was only when the history teacher said that Ripley wasn't the only animal to be knighted that the joking stopped. Apparently, Queen Beatrice of the Netherlands had knighted a penguin in 1980. And, much earlier than that, King Henry VIII had knighted a *dead* animal: a loin (joint) of meat – which is why now a similar joint of meat is known as a "*sir*loin" *(things you learn reading this book, eh?)*. King Henry wasn't keen on pork, which is probably why there are no Sir Pork Chops about today.

Once again, the local newspapers got hold of the story and sploshed it on the front pages, with headlines ranging from:

"HERO DOG TO BE KNIGHTED" – *The Daily Posh*, to:

"TOP HONOUR FOR FART DOG" – The Daily Fib.

Eventually, the day of the investiture came around and the family dressed up in their very best clothes, with Mum in a hat big enough to hide a bus under and Dad in a new cap. They travelled first-class on a coach down to London. The coach driver, though, with passenger safety in mind, had to ask Mum to remove her hat, as he couldn't see the traffic behind in his rearview mirror. Ripley had been washed, trimmed and brushed until he gleamed, and was wearing a new gold collar – well, his old one sprayed, actually. To complement his new cap, Dad had polished his false teeth until they shone like bathroom tiles.

On arrival at Buckingham Palace, they were met by a Lady-in-Waiting – who, despite being asked repeatedly by Jacob, never mentioned what she was waiting for – and were escorted to the Palace's back garden, where there was a huge buffet laid out, and footmen running around giving out drinks, none of which, they noticed, were in cardboard cartons with a straw sticking out.

The buffet didn't suit Jacob or Erin, because there were no chicken nuggets *or* sausage rolls. Ripley was the only dog there, and he got loads of pats and strokes, though most people gave him a wide berth, knowing what he was famous for.

An hour later, everyone was called into the investiture room and given instructions on how to behave in front of Her Very Majesty.

There was to be:

*no muttering, sniffing or coughing…

*no nose-picking or bum-scratching…

*no playing games on mobiles…

and:

*no getting up and going to the toilet, so go before it starts…

When this last one was mentioned, half the people there got up and went, and the proceedings had to be held up until they all got back.

Then, there were instructions on what to do when the Queen shook you by the hand:

*no saying: "That's a nice ring, Your Maj – where'd you get it?"

*definitely no passing wind with excitement (the

instructor gave a sideways glance at Ripley when he said this, and Milly felt compelled to say: "He's cured now.")…

and:

*no attempting to lick the back of her head, just because she's on the front of every postage stamp you've ever bought…

Then, instructions over, they were left to wait, nervously.

Finally, Her Very Majesty arrived on the little stage in front of them all, and excitement ran through the audience. She looked exactly like she did on the telly, only smaller and far more Royal. She was, after all, about as Royal as you could get.

One by one the recipients went up, received their medals and departed stage right, where they were ushered out by one of Her Majesty's ushers. *(Note: an usher's main job is to usher people out, but if he saw anybody chattering in the audience, he'd go over and say: "Ush!")*

Then it was Ripley's turn.

When he was announced, Dad got up and led him to the

Queen (the family were agreed on this, because Dad was the head of the family, but Dad's real reason for doing it was simply so that the Queen could admire his new cap). Ripley sat and the Queen – ignoring Dad's new cap altogether, which rather peeved him – touched the tip of Ripley's right ear with her ceremonial sword. She was just about to touch his left ear with it, when something caught Ripley's eye.

In through the door on the right walked a Corgi! It could have been an Alsatian or a French Bulldog; it didn't matter to Ripley what breed it was – it was a dog, and he ran at it.

As a result, the Queen missed Ripley's left ear and the very heavy sword tipped Her Very Majesty forward, so that she was in danger of falling off the stage. In fact, she *did* fall off the stage, right onto Dad, and lay draped over his left shoulder. Very flustered, Dad set her on her feet again on the stage, and wafted her with his new cap until two big bodyguards rushed over, to check that she was alright. She was – but she was not amused. Neither did she thank Dad for his excellent cap-wafting.

Milly had run after Ripley, who had chased the Corgi into the next room. All the ushers ran after Milly with a finger to their lips, shouting: "Ush! Ush!" Mum, Dad and the twins ran after the ushers, and the ceremony was brought to a halt while the Queen had a blackcurrant Frootshoot to recover.

Despite all that had happened, everything was smoothed over, and the family proudly returned home with Sir Ripley. They were met with newspaper photographers at the station and a throng of neighbours in Gladioli Street, all applauding madly.

THIRTY-SIX
Spain

IT'S A WELL-KNOWN fact that, whenever anyone becomes famous – or, better still, *world* famous, as Ripley now was – most non-famous people want to meet you, and some of them want things from you, like autographs, selfies or one of your socks. Things like that. Others want you to *do* things for them, like open events, sponsor a product, make a charity appearance or even.... *da-dahh!... visit other countries!*

Well, Ripley had already:

*sponsored air fresheners, wet wipes and canine bum spray...

*opened three supermarkets and a home for confused line-dancers...

and – wait for this...

*been invited to a small South Pacific island to fart in front of their queen, 'cos it was thought to bring luck (they refused that one)…

But people kept asking for their time, and they were a nice family who didn't like to say no. They were soon overwhelmed with requests ("overwhelmedness" is not something that anybody likes, and they just wanted to get back to being "whelmed", as soon as possible).

One day, a man calling himself Benny rang, offering to become Ripley's agent – for a fee, of course. He seemed to know what he was talking about. He said he could "field" all their calls and requests, sort out the ones that were "do-able" (which really meant "profitable") and arrange everything for them. "For a fee, of course," he repeated. So, they took him on.

Life did get a bit easier. Benny handled all the bookings, personal appearances, supermarket openings and stuff, as well as the money side of everything, and every month he sent the family what Ripley had earnt – minus his fee. Some months they got as much as twelve-pounds-fifty, while Benny got himself a brand-new, red B.M.W.

This didn't seem quite right to Mum, and she told him so. She found him in his office; he'd just finished polishing all his gold rings, and was dusting off a stack of banknotes when she arrived. He'd actually forgotten who she was, and thought she'd come for an interview to be the office cleaner. When she finally got to say what she had come to say, he appeared most concerned. He apologized until the spittle ran down his chin, and offered to reduce his fee immediately.

"By how much?" asked Mum.

Benny picked up a calculator, put his thoughtful face on (which didn't suit him, but it was the only one he had handy) and punched in numbers, before facing Mum with a beaming smile.

"By a whole 0.0001 percent!" he gleamed.

Now, Mum was good at many things – looking after children, cooking nice dinners, cleaning and all that – but she had never been very good at numbers. In fact, every maths teacher she'd ever had told her that she was "numberlexic", which is the numbers version of *dys*lexic. So, to her Benny's offer sounded a lot and she thanked him.

"Now," said Benny, "I've got a contract for Ripley to go to Spain!"

It seemed that Ripley was very famous in Spain. The Spanish people were amazed that a mere dog could have done all that Ripley had done, and all across the country of Spain, people were trying to train their dog to be like him. It had started as a joke, but a dog food company had turned it into a competition, and announced that the first person to train their dog to *"pedo de orden"* (fart on command) would be crowned *"Rey (or Reya) de Pedo'* – King (or Queen) of the Farts – and win 1000 euros. As a result, the Spanish economy was booming, after over half a million bottles of dog laxative had been sold, one million tonnes of baked beans, plus more poop-a-scoops in one week than had been sold for the last five years!

They wanted Ripley – top celebrity of the year – to trot a circuit of the bullring in Madrid, at the opening of the bullfighting season. It was worth a lot of money, Benny said.

"How much?" asked Mum.

"Errr... two thousand pounds," said Benny.

But he mumbled it in a way that made her suspicious, so she asked to see the contract. Benny didn't want to show her, but she insisted – she did this by grabbing his tie and hauling him across his desk. In this subtle way, she was able to point out to him that the contract said *twelve* thousand pounds, not *two* thousand! Once again, Benny was super-apologetic, blaming his glasses, the bad lighting, the weather, and saying he hadn't seen the number one. Mum slid him back in his chair and said that the family and Ripley would go, so long as all their airfares were paid and they were put up in a swanky hotel. Benny's mouth drooped at the corners, but he agreed.

Mum went home happy, to tell them all to pack their sun cream.

THIRTY-SEVEN
Bully

THE ARRIVALS HALL at Madrid's Barajas airport was packed with Spanish Ripley well-wishers when they got there. Some had placards saying things like *"VIVA RIPLEY!"* or *"AZOTE LAS LADRONES"* (*"SCOURGE OF THE ROBBERS"*). One placard said, *"DAMEMOS UN PEDO,"* which meant, more or less, *"SHOW US WHAT YOU CAN DO"*. But Ripley, still on his meat-free diet, couldn't have done so even if he had been able to read Spanish, which he couldn't, and I don't know a dog that can.

Their hotel was like an Arab castle… after a huge battle had been fought! It was comfortable enough, but the rusty water coming out of the taps, and the patter of cockroach feet in the night-time, caused them to make a mental note not to deal with Benny anymore.

The next day was the start of the bullfighting season, when Ripley was to make his appearance and circle the bullring before the first fight. This was the biggest booking that Benny had ever done for anybody – except for when he had booked a juggler at a very posh wedding, whose juggling clubs had smashed the wedding cake to bits and given the groom a black eye, after which the groom gave the juggler a black eye. With an eye to enhancing his reputation, Benny desperately wanted people to know that he was the brains behind the Ripley trip. So, what did he do? He jumped into his big, red B.M.W. and drove to Madrid.

At the start of the ceremony, trumpets were sounded and Ripley padded into the arena, accompanied by Jacob and Erin, to tremendous applause. Most of the crowd were waving white handkerchiefs, but there were a few Union Jacks, which were like big, multicoloured handkerchiefs, I suppose. And there was more than one of those contraptions called a "kazoo", which makes a noise very like a bottom burp when you blow it.

Ripley behaved himself perfectly, and did the perimeter walk with his head high, his tail wagging and, of course, his tongue hanging out. People threw flowers and money, and

Erin was kept busy picking them all up. There were also dog collars thrown, with lady-dog names on them, like "Pepita", "Angelina" or "Lola". Some women even held their lady dogs up so that Ripley could see them, and blew kisses from the dogs' mouths with their free hand. Some people, eh?

Toward the end of the walk, who should jump into the ring, wearing a bright-red suit to match his bright-red car, but agent Benny! He began to take all the applause, striding about with a big grin and his arms in the air. In bold, black letters on his back were the words: *"RIPLEY PROMOTIONS – RING +44 720 6391."*

Suddenly more trumpets were blown and, just as suddenly, stewards were anxiously ushering Ripley and the kids through the barrier and behind the ring. Benny was somewhere near the centre of the ring, still jumping about and pointing over his shoulder, at the advertisement on his back, when the first bull of the day was released from its pen.

It pounded into the ring like a tank on legs, bulging muscles gleaming with sweat, blasting hot air noisily from its nostrils, and two huge, curved horns glinting in the sun. It looked around fiercely for something – anything – to kill, and the first thing it saw that *might* be worth killing was Benny!

And Benny saw the bull.

His eyes bulged and his red trousers went a darker shade, as he quietly peed himself in fright. Then he screamed, turned and ran. He headed for the first escape route he saw: the two big (but closed) doors which led out onto the street. Mr. Bull gave a fearsome snort and pounded after him. One quick-thinking steward, who saw what was about to happen, ran to the doors, swung one of them open and hid behind it.

Standing outside the doors was Benny's big, bright-red B.M.W. Benny ran to it and just managed to jump into the driver's seat, as the bull arrived. Mr. Bull wasn't going to let a mere car get in his way, though; he rammed it good and hard, shattering the windows. Then he backed off and rammed it again, both horns going through the bodywork. In fact, he rammed it so many times that, when he'd tired himself out and trotted out into the street, scattering people as he went, he left behind a Benny with wet pants, blubbering with fright, and a car that looked like it had been attacked by an Apache fighter helicopter.

With the money they got (Benny was in no condition to pick it up), the family decided to book themselves into a better hotel and stay a few more days in the sunshine.

Dad was particularly pleased, because he had filmed all the goings-on, and he knew that his favourite magazine *Believe It Or Not* would pay him nicely for the footage.

Everywhere they went, Ripley was recognized and lauded. They spent six lovely days being pampered, before heading back to blustery old England.

THIRTY-EIGHT

Siege

TO THE SURPRISE of everyone, out of the blue came a call from Inspector Lector. To the disbelief of everybody, he had now been promoted to *Chief* Inspector.

This made him Chief Inspector Lector of the Hostage Sector.

Unknown to only a few people, before he had joined the police he had been, for a short time, a church minister, which made him Chief Inspector Lector, ex-rector, of the Hostage Sector.

He had also, in his past, been working for a gas company as a leak detector, but I'll let you, dear reader, work that one out.

Regarding the surprise of his promotion, there was a rumour that the company which made Jammy Dodgers – surprisingly known as the Jammy Dodger Company – was owned by the cousin of the son of the father of the man whose job it was to decide who was promoted in the Police Force. Whether this is true or not, no one will ever know, but since his promotion it was a fact that Chief Inspector Lector gave everyone who visited his office, as well as a cup of tea, a plateful of Jammy Dodgers, and expected that person (or persons) to scoff at least six before getting down to business. Not only that, but in the police canteen he made sure that each table had at least two platefuls, which were topped up every ten minutes by the serving staff.

Anyway, this call from him came as a big surprise and – from what Mum heard, between the crunches of biscuit over the phone – caused the family to gather, to discuss the implications of what was said.

What Lector wanted was Ripley (whom he only referred to now as Dog 27) to come out of retirement for one particular purpose, and that was in order to resolve one particular hostage situation, which had already been going on for a whole week. The incident had been in all the papers and on the telly.

Three clowns – not real clowns, just three fellers dressed as clowns – had tried to rob a joke shop, armed with pistols.

Now, if they had been *real* clowns, they would have had the owner of the shop helpless with laughter long enough to rob him. But being *fake* clowns, the owner had been able to disable them with itching powder, and followed up by throwing half a dozen rubber spiders at them.

A passer-by, noticing all this, had the sense to call the police and now, according to Lector, the clowns were refusing to come out of the shop, and were holding the shopkeeper, his family and two customers at gunpoint.

Both Dad and Jacob were against letting Ripley be used, arguing that it wouldn't be a good thing to reactivate his system now that it was under control. Mum and the girls agreed, but felt so sorry for the hostages in the shop that they felt guilty, knowing that they only had to say yes to Lector, to free them from their week-long misery.

The other problem, of course, was that they were a nice family who didn't like to say no.

So, after four cups of strong tea each, and a lot of real thinking, they said yes.

Handler Jim came to collect Ripley that very day, and Ripley was so happy to see him that he draped himself, like a big, woolly scarf, around Jim's neck as he sat on the settee, and slobbered all down Jim's left arm.

The "Joke Shop Siege", as it had become known, could have been resolved without much fuss, if only Inspector Lector had realized that it wasn't a robbery attempt at all. The joke shop owner had hired the three men to dress as clowns, in a publicity stunt to attract customers; the itching powder and the rubber spiders had all been a part of the stunt. However, Lector, anxious to show his Inspectorability, had hemmed the "robbers" in using two police vans, positioned in a V shape in front of the shop. He had filled the space in the "V" with heavily armed Hit Squad snipers, plus he had a man in each of the vans, with "tank-buster" bazookas poking out of the side windows.

Lector, once again with his cap back to front and a mad look in his eye, had been on his megaphone every ten minutes for a week, ordering the petrified clowns to come out, little realizing that the clowns were too frightened to move. They became even more frightened when they saw the Challenger #Mark 2 tank which Lector had requested, rumbling up the street.

Ripley's arrival at the scene was met with cheers from the armed police who, by this time, were fed up to the back teeth of having had to point heavy guns at the shop for a whole week – minus tea breaks – whilst in a kneeling position. None of them could either scratch their bums or even wipe their noses on their sleeves, without Lector screaming at them to hold their positions. Lector gave Jim a long, boring brief on how he expected the situation to be resolved.

"They *are* armed!" he said, and the way his right eyebrow shot up showed that he meant it. He then commanded them to proceed.

Jim and Ripley weaved their way through the (really fed up) armed men, ending up at the shop door.

"Careful," whispered one policeman, "they've got water pistols."

"But the inspector said they were armed," replied Jim.

The man just shrugged and rolled his eyes to Heaven.

Jim took from his bag the piece of prime fillet steak that Ripley would need in order to do his duty, and unwrapped it. At the same time, one of the clowns peered at him through the window and put a note up to the glass which read: *"HELP US!"* He followed this up with a pathetic squirt from his water pistol. Jim looked from the frightened clowns to the meat in his hands, wrapped it up again and put it back in his pocket. Ripley, by this time, was knocking with his tail, on the door that he knew he was meant to enter.

Just then, Lector's voice came through the megaphone: "GET DOG 27 INSIDE, IMMEDIATELY!!"

This was followed by a distinct *CRUNCH!* as he stuffed another Jammy Dodger into his gob, before switching off.

Jim motioned to the clown inside to unlock the door, which he seemed pleased to do (though clowns always look pleased, right?), then Jim turned to Ripley.

"You can do this, Rippers," he whispered. "Just show 'em what you're made of." And he ushered Ripley inside.

Ripley entered, tail wagging, tongue hanging and frisked about, going from person to person for a stroke, paying particular attention to the clowns, because of the permanent painted smiles on their faces.

Immediately all the people in there – clowns, customers and the shopkeeper's family – relaxed, sensing that their ordeal was over.

The armed men outside, seeing this, sighed a sigh of relief and lowered their weapons, as did the guys with the bazookas in the vans. Seeing this, the tank, which had its gun trained on the shop, angled the weapon away.

But this wasn't the way in which Inspector Lector had wanted the siege to end, and he knew that the situation was slipping from his grasp. He went bonkers!

"Keep your weapons trained on the target!" he bellowed. "ON THE TARGET!!"

But nobody was taking any notice of him now and, as the shop door opened and Ripley exited, followed by everyone in there, the whole attack force stood and applauded in relief.

"OBEY MY ORDERS!!" bellowed Lector's panicky voice, two octaves higher than usual. "Obey! Obey!" he continued, then added, pathetically: "Jammy Dodgers for everybody! Free!! No charge!!! *OBEY!!!!*" He was jumping up and down on his car bonnet now.

"FIRE! OPEN FIRE!!! Do you hear me?! Shoot!!! Shoot them all!!"

Then he began blubbering, his eyeballs protruding, and sat on the bonnet of his car making bloopy noises, with his fingers strumming his lips.

In less than ten minutes an ambulance had arrived, and he was carried away, singing:

"Jammy Dodgers... Jammy Dodgers... Jammy Dodgers... I cry.

"If I don't have Jammy Dodgers, I know I will die."

THIRTY-NINE

Love

A HOUSE ACROSS the road – number 97 – which had been empty for ages, became occupied by a family: a mum and dad, a girl about Jacob and Erin's age, called Daisy, and a dog. The dog looked almost exactly like Ripley in every way, except that it was a "she", and she was called Lula.

Whoever's turn it was to walk Ripley would sometimes meet Daisy, with Lula, on the common behind the supermarket. Daisy was a bright, happy girl who loved dogs and loved life itself, and soon they all became good friends.

So did the dogs. Ripley loved having someone like himself to play with and, when the two of them weren't in Ripley's garden, they would romp and run off together across the common, when being walked. Ripley and Lula looked so alike that, from a distance, it was impossible to say who was who.

For some reason, Jacob began taking Ripley out even

when it wasn't his turn. He could be found staring out of the front window at number 97, until he saw Daisy going out with Lula, then he would dash to take Ripley out as well. Ripley didn't mind how often he was taken out – he would play with Lula all day, if he could – and Jacob didn't mind because, when the two dogs ran off over the meadow, he could sit and talk with Daisy, whom he had taken a particular shine to.

Things went on like this for maybe six months or so, in sun, rain and snow (once in fog, and twice when it was really windy, too), and Lula and Daisy became almost like members of the family. Daisy would spend time at the Wigglesworth-Winterbottoms and vice versa *(that's Latin for "the other way round")*. Choccy biccies had a lot to do with it: each Mum had a tinful.

Ripley and Lula became really firm friends, and loved each other's company, but it soon became clear who the boss was in this relationship. If there was somewhere that Lula wanted Ripley to be, she would grab his ear in her mouth and lead him there – and he'd go, meekly. Similarly, if they felt like a snack between feed times, they'd go to

Ripley's shed, where Ripley would operate his food doo-dah and deliver a portion to Lula, and then – only then – one for himself. They came to know each other's likes and habits, and though nobody had told her (and she wouldn't have understood if they had done), Lula seemed to know that Ripley never ate any meat of any kind. She, of course, was a carnivore, and when she was eating what Daisy gave her, she was very careful not to let Ripley take any – but, being Ripley, that didn't stop him from trying.

Erin noticed all of this and became quite certain that they were in love. In fact, she asked Mum if dogs were allowed to get married and, if so, did she know anybody – maybe a doggy vicar – who might do it? Mum was baking a cheese and strawberry pie at the time (strawberries because she had no radishes, which were the same colour), so she didn't take her seriously. So, Erin sent an email to the Kennel Club, an organization which registers dogs and looks after their welfare:

"Dear Kennel Club,
My dog and the one that lives across the road

are madly in love, and would like to get married. Please can you arrange it?

   Yours sincerely,

   Erin Wigglesworth-Winterbottom."

The Kennel Club replied, saying:

"Dear Miss Wigglesworth-Winterbottom,

   Don't be daft. How many married dogs do you know?"

Then:

"However, it is not unknown for weddings to take place between dogs, although it is extremely rare, and anybody who does it needs to be a lady – usually a large, very rich lady – with two poodles, who has little else to occupy her mind.

   Yours sincerely,

   Winifred Wagtail."

Dad was in complete agreement with this. "Can't imagine two big beefy Rottweilers getting married, can you?" he postured.

So, Erin dropped the subject, from a general lack of interest.

Her interest flared up again, one day soon after, when Jacob and Daisy arrived back from the common, with two empty leads and a couple of worried frowns.

"What did I tell you?" Erin cried. "They've eloped! They've run off to spend the rest of their lives together!"

"They've run off, alright," returned Jacob, "and got themselves lost!"

Daisy's dad, a big, beefy bloke that you wouldn't choose to argue with, considering the scar across his face, but a nice enough character usually, wasn't happy and blamed Ripley.

"I knew he'd be a bad influence on our Lula," he growled, then turned to Dad; "wot you gonna do about getting her back?"

Dad drew himself up to his full height, looked him straight in the kneecaps and said: "L... leave it to me... err... Mr. Smith... err, Bruno... I... I'll see to it."

So, it was cars-out-and-search, both families. Long hours driving around streets, searching parks and Dad dodging scowls from Big Bruno Smith whenever their paths crossed. Daisy and Jacob were on the naughty step for not looking after them properly, and a fortune was spent on big mugs of tea and choccy biccies, to keep their spirits up between searches.

Mum and Daisy's mum, Gloria, went to the Animal Rescue, to see if they'd been handed in, and were met with:

"'Handed in'? Wot you fink this is, lost property?"

Then a manager rolled up and said:

"Sorry about that – can't get the staff. We'll let you know if they turn up. Give us a description."

"Cockerpoos. Two. Black," said Gloria, a woman of few words, but with a look that could scour a pan.

Then off they both went.

Milly, Jacob and the two dads went to the police station, where Bruno Smith raised the possibility of dog theft, which Dad hadn't considered, and it kick-started his Conspiracy Theory Syndrome. Within ten minutes he had compiled ten theories, in which the dogs had been snaffled, sold on, were probably abroad right now and, finally, that they could be in China, which is a nation full of people who regularly have *DOG FOR DINNER!* However, when Bruno Smith waved a huge fist under his nose, he calmed down and kept his theories to himself.

By the day's end, the dogs were still missing, despite Jacob sprinting the full length of a street when he spotted two black dogs, sitting side by side on a wall. Jacob's eyesight had never been the best in the world, so when he got there, panting and sweating, to find it was two black plastic bags full of grass cuttings, waiting for the bin man, he decided, under his breath, to think about visiting an optician.

Night fell and still no dogs found. Both families went to their respective homes, sad and tired, but fully prepared to continue the search the next day.

Sitting gloomily in the house, with no T.V. and glum stares at the fire, Erin had a thought: the dogs *were* in love, she was sure of it. Nobody recognized it but her. She thought a bit more, then got up, grabbed a torch from the drawer and went out to Ripley's shed.

She'd been right all along. Love was the reason!

There, on Ripley's cushion, lay Ripley and Lula, fast asleep. Ripley had his paw around Lula's shoulder.

FORTY

News

MAYBE A MONTH after the being "lost" incident, Daisy came over to visit, and she had a very serious face on – a face that she hadn't had on since they'd known her. It was a concerned kind of face, and it was obvious there was something on her mind, apart from her hat. She kept herself very quiet, and when she refused a choccy biccy, they knew it was serious. They had to ask her what the matter was.

"It's Lula," she said.

"What is it? What's up with her?" they asked, anxiously.

Daisy paused.

"She's pregnant."

And her "serious" face broke into a broad smile. "She's going to have puppies!"

Every mouth fell open.

"That's wonderful!" stuttered Mum. "Who's the

father?"

Daisy paused, her eyebrows raised.

Mum twigged the look. "Not... not Ripley?!"

FORTY-ONE

Sausage Rolls

WELL, THE EXCITEMENT of Daisy's news was beyond anything they had known before.

It beat:

*the day that Princess Anne visited Mum's school dinner-hall, and ate one of her sausage rolls…

*the time that Dad saw Anne Boleyn's ghost filling up at the petrol station (it was a woman on the way to a fancy-dress party)…

and, was better than:

*their visit to Lapland (before they realized they were in the grotto at the supermarket)…

"When will they be here?" asked a breathless Erin.

"In about ten weeks," answered Daisy, equally breathless.

"How many? How many?"

Daisy shrugged: "Who knows?"

"What'll we call them?"

It took a whole week to come up with a list. Suggestions ranged from:

*Chips (but not Fish)…

and:

*Ringo (but not Paul or John or George)…

to:

*Bubbles (too soppy for Jacob)…

*Rover (too many Rovers in the world)…

*Spot (but they weren't likely to *have* spots)…

*Keith (really?!)…

*Elvis…

*Lady Gaga…

*Ant *and* Dec…

and:

*Jaws…

Dad wanted either E.T. or R2D2, though he would have settled for Chewbacca.

Ripley knew that something was going on, from all the excitement and all the hugs he was getting, and he searched everybody's face for clues. He didn't know what "congratulations" meant, but it sounded nice because of the way it was said to him.

The news that Ripley was to be a father was very well received by his fans, and there came a number of offers to buy the pups at very high prices – but, of course, nobody had any plans to sell them. The newspapers ran the story, and he got a congratulations message from Her Very Majesty.

The two families (Ripley's and Lula's) decided they'd hold a "puppy shower" for them, which is a bit like a "baby shower", only different. In baby showers, you shower the parents-to-be with presents for the baby-to-come, but with a puppy shower you shower the parents-to-be with presents for the… errm… for the puppies-to-come… So, forget what I just said about it being different, 'cos it's not. The parents-to-be were there, of course, wondering what all the fuss was about.

The two of them sat together on the Settee of Honour and, throughout the day of the puppy shower, they had so many biscuits given to them that they thought they were in Biscuit Heaven. There were fig rolls, too (Ripley's fave) and – *watch out!* – SAUSAGE ROLLS (but only for human consumption). Well-wishers kept arriving at the door and each one brought a present. The happy couple got:

*75 dog leads (all colours of the rainbow)…

*86 food bowls: 43 blue and 43 pink (all empty)…

*a variety of collars (none of which would ever fit a puppy)…

*enough blankets to see an Eskimo through the winter…

*18 dog baskets (including one so big that puppies would get lost in it and never be seen again)…

*4 red cushions (all heart-shaped)…

and:

*56 dog tags, all blank except for one, which had spaces for name, address, nationality, ethnicity, religious preference, mobile number of owner, mobile number of dog, birth sign, star sign and social security number. It was as big as a very big dinner plate and should, in all reality, have been worn by a dinosaur…

All this might give you an idea of how many people were in the house – so many that some had to sit outside and look in through the windows; a few even sat on the wall across the street, and watched through binoculars.

Queenie Renée was there in a ballgown, a tiara balanced on top of her wig, shoving her hand in people's faces for them to kiss it. Jacob kept clear of her. He wasn't into kissing. Not only would he never kiss a woman's hand, but he would never, *ever* kiss the hand of a feller pretending to be a woman, who was pretending to be a queen. *Yeeeeerk!*

Everything was going well. Ripley and Lula were sitting side by side on their settee, when someone who should have known better came along, and placed a plateful of sausage rolls on a table next to them.

Ripley smelled meat!

He hadn't had meat for a long, long time...

Lula smelled it, too, and when she leaned over and snaffled a couple, he didn't see why he shouldn't do the same.

But Ripley had six!

Then they exchanged a guilty glance and finished off the whole plateful between them.

Five minutes later, Milly was passing when she spotted the plate, with nothing on it but crumbs, and spotted Ripley and Lula all crumbed up, licking their chops and looking very satisfied.

She went pale, then quickly went over and talked quietly with Mum. Mum's eyes went wide and her mouth sagged.

Now, in every doctor's *Medical Dictionary* it says that wide eyes and a saggy mouth are sure signs of shock, panic, anxiety and horror. Mum had them all.

She was:

*shocked…

*panicked…

*anxious…

and:

*horrified…

plus:

*she had a runny nose, 'cos she had a cold…

She also had a mental picture of what could happen. With about 10,000 people in the house, if Ripley "performed" people could be killed in the rush to get out!

She called Dad and the children to her and, very quietly, told them what had happened.

"We have to evacuate this place quickly, quietly and

without causing panic," she said.

"No problem, Mum," said Milly, "just tell 'em you've got some of your pies coming out of the oven."

"I'm serious!" said Mum.

"So am I!" replied Milly.

For the next half hour, the five of them went from group to group, trying to persuade people, as politely as possible, that it was time to go.

Some of the excuses for going were:

*the dogs were getting tired…

*_Coronation Street_ was about to start and they might miss it…

*a tornado was forecast in the next two minutes…

and:

*the roof was about to fall in….

Despite all this, hardly anybody left, and each minute that passed made it more likely that the worst was going to happen. Dad, who always had his phone on speed dial to ring 999, just in case he had to, now had the phone out, with his finger hovering over the "call" button in readiness.

When Ripley left his chair and stood in the middle of the

room, with a certain look on his face, Jacob thought he recognized the signs. He jumped on a chair and shouted:

"Listen, everybody!"

No response.

He picked up a sausage roll and lobbed it at a big lady with an even bigger voice. It hit her in the ear, and her whoop of surprise turned everybody's head.

"LISTEN!" repeated Jacob.

They listened.

"Ripley's loaded and he's about to go off!"

Well, the panic that Mum had been trying to avoid happened.

Every doorway was jammed, people crawled out of windows, a dozen ran upstairs, and the back garden suddenly looked like Trafalgar Square on a Friday night! The hall doorway came off its hinges and was carried away in the crowd. A jug of petunias crashed to the floor, making a perfect skid-grid, and legs flew up in the air.

Queenie strode about, magnificent in her ballgown, but with her tiara over one eye, trilling: "Don't panic... don't panic! Queenie's here!"

Luckily, only one person – an elderly lady – was trampled, and she recovered quickly, after two large brandies and a packet of Joosyfruits as compensation.

Strangely, by the time the house was cleared – about thirty seconds – Ripley still hadn't disgraced himself, and after another hour he had convinced everybody that he wasn't going to.

"Strange," said Dad, as everyone expected Dad would, "very strange." And he went off to consult his book *Why Expected Happenings Don't Happen.*

"Do y'suppose he's, like, completely cured?" asked Erin.

"Who knows?" said Mum. "Perhaps time will tell."

Time didn't tell.

In fact, time never said a word all that evening and well into the next day.

It was the day after that when time told – and what time had to say wasn't very nice at all…

FORTY-TWO
Supervet

AT THE TIME, nobody realized that Ripley's surprising behaviour at the puppy shower was the first indication that he was not well. When something doesn't happen that you know perfectly well *should* happen, you do wonder why...

The following day, he seemed to be in slow motion and disinterested. The day after that, he spent a lot of his time sleeping in his shed, and the first flickers of real concern seeped into everyone's mind.

His listlessness continued, and each day it seemed to be worse. He wasn't eating much, and he began to refuse to go for walks. Even visits from Lula seemed to spark little interest and, about two months into Lula's pregnancy, it reached the point where he became almost immobile. On the Tuesday of that week, he was lying half-heartedly in the back garden with Lula, and on the Wednesday he was so listless that he just lay around all day.

"Not like him at all," Dad muttered, and after the family had convinced him that Ripley couldn't possibly have been cursed by some deeply offended African witch doctor, he went off to consult his *Famous Dog Remedies* book.

Ripley was still the same a week later, when he went off his food altogether. Mum tried him with his favourite things – even strings of tasty sausages – and Jacob gave him extra dollops of tomato sauce but, try as they may, nobody could get him to eat anything *at all*.

It wasn't long before he began to look thin, the glossiness went out of his coat and a weakness overtook him.

The vet saw him and decided that the cause lay in his unusual and unique intestinal set-up, but just couldn't pinpoint what the exact problem was. They were at a complete loss as to what to do. He didn't appear to be in any pain, but one thing was sure: they couldn't let him go on like this; it was breaking their hearts.

The family had seen, on television, the marvellous programme about the *Super Vet*, a genius of a man called Noel Fitzpatrick, and it was Mum's suggestion that they took Ripley to him. An appointment was made and the whole family went.

Daisy and Little John followed in Little John's Mum's car. It was a long drive, and when they got there Ripley was so weak that they had to carry him into the surgery.

Although Noel Supervet didn't have a big *"S"* on his t-shirt (neither did he wear a cloak or his underpants over tights), he most certainly was a *super* vet, and there wasn't anything that he didn't know about animals – especially dogs. He had, of course, heard of Ripley – who hadn't? – and said that it would be an honour to treat him, at no cost whatsoever.

X-rays came first, which confirmed the previous vet's findings that every organ in Ripley's body was at least twice the size of those in any ordinary dog.

"If we were allowed to eat dogs," said Noel Supervet, "his liver alone would keep a family of four fed for a whole month."

None of this was good news and the worry mounted.

Noel Supervet asked if he could keep Ripley for a week for observation, to try to figure out what the problem really was and how he might treat it. Of course, the family agreed. They left him there and went home, as worried a bunch of people as there ever had been.

It was the longest week of their lives – even longer than when Erin was in hospital with tonsillitis, and that was *two* weeks. Even longer than the vicar's sermon, on the odd occasion that they went to church – and that lasted at least a *month*!

Noel Supervet rang them at the end of the week and, without saying anything about Ripley's condition, asked them to pick him up. There was something about Noel Supervet's tone of voice which made them worry even more – if that were possible!

When they got there, he had some devastating news, saying that Ripley's condition had worsened, and he was afraid there was nothing more that could be done for him. Ripley's condition, he said, was terminal.

It took more than a few minutes for what Noel Supervet had said to sink in, but when it did a great sadness descended on everyone, like a black cloud hiding the sun, and they all shed the first of many tears to come. No words were spoken, just "thank you" to Noel Supervet for his help, before they carried Ripley to the car and made him comfortable for the long ride back. The only sounds on the long journey were sniffles and sobs.

Over the next six weeks, Ripley got gradually weaker, but was still able to wag a feeble tail when someone bent to stroke him.

On a cold November day, snow lying thinly on the ground, the family dozing miserably by the fire, they had a visitor. It was Daisy, along with Little John, and they had something with them: a basket. In the basket, lined with a blanket, they had brought the three little, black, curly Cockerpoo puppies which Lula had given birth to, only an hour earlier.

Everyone made a fuss, but really Ripley was the one that needed to see them – Ripley, their father.

Ripley's eyes brightened when they held the puppies to him. He licked them almost joyously and his tail wagged, as it used to.

But the effort tired him out and he had to lie back down. And shortly after, with the tiniest of sighs, Ripley slipped away into Doggy Heaven…

FORTY-THREE
After Ripley

THE PASSING OF a much-loved pet can be a traumatic experience, and often takes a long time to get over – if ever.

Ripley was such a *special* pet that his loss hit the family hard, and they grieved for him every single day, as did Little John, Daisy and Lula. Lula in particular, because no one could give her an explanation for what had happened, and she consoled herself with her puppies. Nobody could believe that he was no longer there. Like all people who grieve for a lost loved one, the family went through all the well-known stages of grieving: shock, sadness, disbelief, then anger and finally (but only eventually) acceptance.

The word went out to the now international Fan Club (R.I.F.C.) and tributes, flowers and cards began to arrive from every part of the world. There were lots of tears – so many that they decided to clear the living room floor of used tissues only at the end of each day, to save them the bother of bending down all the time to pick them up. The sadness of it all meant that the only sounds in the house all day were sniffles and sobs – so much so that when Erin tried to say something, she found that she'd almost forgotten how to speak; it had been so long since she had done so. Initially, they all refused to admit to themselves that it had happened, but they only had to look at Ripley's empty basket to remind them that it was true. He was gone.

Then came the *"if only"*s, when they blamed themselves (though, thankfully, not each other) for bringing about his death:

* *"If only we had sought treatment earlier…"*

* *"If only his diet hadn't been interrupted by the robbers, and then his police work…"*

* *"If only… if only… if only…"*

It wasn't until after they put him to rest that the pain began to ease a little. They chose a patch of back garden that he had particularly liked. Dad made a special box to put him in, along with his favourite toys, and Milly made a little headstone in pottery class at school, with the inscription:

"RIPLEY – NEVER FORGOTTEN."

Then they stuck their fave photo of him on it.

Everyone wanted to attend the little ceremony, but they decided that, apart from family, only Little John, Daisy and Jim his handler should be there. But, outside in the street crowds had gathered: friends, neighbours and almost every member of the Fan Club. Some had travelled great distances: two families had come from India, three from Australia and a group of six Chinese people. All had brought flowers and gifts.

They laid him to rest to the tune of "How Much is That Doggy in the Window?" (*which, dear reader, you can access on your favourite music app*), then they allowed everyone into the garden, so that they could walk past the grave and pay their respects. All of this was recorded by television cameras, and relayed the following evening on both the national and local news.

What really helped at this sad time was the joy of having Lula and Ripley's puppies. They were a sheer blessing.

Milly, Jacob and Erin began to spend loads more time over at number 97, just to be with them, 'cos it eased the pain of losing their beloved Ripley. Names for the pups had been agreed: Meany, Miney and Mo. Mo had the pinkest of pink noses and a tail which, like his dad's, never stopped wagging.

One rainy night, maybe two weeks later, the family were sitting at home, playing Monopoly without much enthusiasm (Milly was winning, Jacob had been in jail for half an hour and Erin was nearly skint), when a knock came on the door. It was Daisy. She joined them and, being the bright girl that she was, had Jacob out of jail in two ticks and had built up Erin's bank balance, which raised her spirits no end.

But it was when Daisy opened her coat, allowing a little head to pop out, that spirits, for the first time in a month, went through the roof. She had brought Mo.

MO! With his two bright eyes, and the tip of his little pink nose snuffling in curiosity.

"He's for you," said Daisy.

"For us?!"

"Yep, he`s old enough to leave his mother now, and there's no one else I'd like to have him more than yourselves. He's the one who looks most like Ripley."

Daisy had thought it all out and come to a decision, which meant the world to everyone who had loved Ripley most. She had given Meany to Little John and kept Miney for herself.

The difference that little soul made to their lives was amazing!

Mo made them laugh so much, and gave them as much joy as his father had. He fitted in perfectly and soon had the run of the house, the garden and, best of all, Ripley's shed. Strangely enough, he seemed to know exactly how to operate his dad's food and water contraption, and knew, also, how to switch the heater both on *and* off. Suddenly, life was worth living once more.

Mo grew quickly, and by the end of the summer he was already more than half as big as Ripley had been. If they had tried, none of the family would have been able to count how many times one of them said: "It's just like having Ripley back again."

And it was... exactly the same!

One evening, in the autumn, the family were sitting in

front of a warm fire, with Mo sprawled on the rug watching *Falling About On Ice*, when the television began to flicker. They all looked at each other apprehensively, remembering the occasion when that had happened before…

Milly just had time to mutter a disbelieving, "No!" before, in the next moment, they fled for the door, hands over their mouths, noses pinched, leaving Mo to wonder where they'd all gone.

Once outside on the front lawn, horror gave way to mirth, and they laughed louder and longer than a pack of hyenas at a comedy concert…

The End

Acknowledgements

Firstly, many thanks to Matt McAvoy at MJV Literary Author Services, without whose help this book would not be in its joined-up state.

Also to Tim Bacon and Kelly Dodd for the excellent art work on the cover. Ripley says woof!

Thanks to the real-life Ripley (and his real-life bum) for his generous, flatulent encouragement.

And, lastly, appreciation must go to the Birkenhead Institute of Fartology, whose work in the fields of Niffs, Pongs and Silent Ones was invaluable.

By the Same Author

Brog the Stoop.

Brog 2 Retribution

The Year of the Phial

And for younger readers:

Accrington Stanley – Hero of the People

Accrington Stanley and the Coach Trip

Accrington Stanley Saves Bluebell Wood

Printed in Great Britain
by Amazon